LIVING THINGS

LIVING THINGS
SHORT TALES OF SCIENCE FICTION AND DYSTOPIA

by
Jackie Gamber

Edited by
Cover Art by
Interior Design by
Ellen Kjiersten Gamber

Written by
Jackie Gamber

Contents

LIVING THINGS

Freak Museum

After eleven miles, hobbled by the stone in his shoe, Simon sat to rest. The silt of the Midwest Desert was placid, but he could taste a storm on the horizon; he would have to reach the Iowa border by dusk. He shook out the rock from his left shoe and switched it to his right. Then he stood, pulled his moldy cloak tighter, and limped on.

A flare of barking sounded behind him, rising over an outlying dune. He felt a rumble through the ground, and he turned to spot a dog sled overtaking him. Slathering dog mouths yapped. Paws wrapped in Velcro kicked up gray silt like smoke.

"Ho, friend," called the driver over the noise, yanking the dogs to a stop. He pulled down a cloth from his face, revealing the bulging eye in his forehead, the twisted septum of his nose. "So you're the footprints from Aledo."

"I'm on to Muscatine," said Simon, hunching his spine, hiding his face against his shoulder.

A dog snarled, curling back fuzzy lips from toothless gums. Other dogs circled, nudging against their leather bindings, their faces puckered; eyes, nose and muzzle curled inward like slices of sun-dried lemons.

Their master tossed them boiled suet with his shrunken fingers. "Settle," he said, and then offered a slab of fat toward Simon.

Simon shook his head.

"Long way to Muscatine," said the man, sucking at the pearly suet on his finger nubs. "Got room for a rider, if you're wishing to beat the storm."

He didn't often receive kind gestures. "Thank you," said Simon, and made for the sled before the man could change his mind.

The man wiped his fingers against his trousers, and then took up the reins while Simon nestled into parcels and crates. "Sleep if you want," he said. "I got no intention to harm."

In all of Simon's travels, if ever there was a man he longed to believe, it was the sled driver. Still, as the excited dogs lurched and lumbered their way across the endless Midwest Desert, Simon kept his eyes open.

They reached Muscatine just as the air turned hot. Drawing near, Simon could see structures of brick and stone; and metal, shining through gaping wounds in ruined buildings like skeleton bones. A second city of haphazard canvas tents lined streets and wrapped the buildings like a knitted shawl around elderly shoulders. He sat up.

"First time to an old city?" asked the driver.

"No, sir," said Simon. He'd seen plenty, from Albany to Altoona to Kokomo, following caravans of carnivals and their sideshows, searching. Endlessly searching.

"What brings you across the Midwest in the middle of storm season?"

Simon mentally filed through his lies, trying them on. "Carnival work," he said, finally deciding to mix in some truth.

"Ah," said the driver, smiling behind his mask, gathering it into curving wrinkles with his lips.

A gust blew suddenly savage, carrying the dampness of the Mississippi Canal, and Simon tasted mud. The dogs turned their backs to the wind, jerking the sled to a stop.

"That's it for the boys, then. They won't go any farther, with that storm picking up," said the man.

Simon disentangled himself from the cargo.

"You got some barter?" the man asked.

Simon had nothing but decrepit rags for clothing and an empty stomach.

"Here," said the man, tugging down his mask again, and withdrawing nails from his pocket. "Steel will get you a tent and a meal. Take them."

Simon gratefully reached. Gauze unwrapped from his hand, offering a glance at his lanky, jointed fingers.

The man recoiled. His eye widened, and then squinted.

Simon quickly restored the gauze, covering his unblemished skin. "Please—"

"What kind of work do you do for the carnival?"

"I'm searching," said Simon.

"Rumor chaser?"

Simon hated that term. What he chased wasn't rumor.

"You don't look like a scientist," said the man, his eye studying Simon. "More like a sideshow, if you know what I mean."

"I don't want trouble," said Simon.

"I don't intend to give you any," said the man. He offered the nails again. "I hear the carnival in Muscatine's got more than the usual phony bones and wax hands. You heard about it?"

"The Freak Museum?" Simon took the nails.

"No, no," said the man, waving. "Just a carnival." He bent to unhitch his sled, and then paused. "That museum gossip, you don't believe in all that do you?"

Just a legend, people said. Ghost stories. About scientists studying more than exhumed fossil bones, more than archaeological leftovers. In a mysterious laboratory in the middle of somewhere, scientists studied people—living, breathing humans—with dysmelial four-fingered hands and opposable thumbs; faces disfigured with double eyes; feet with five, flexible toes.

Did Simon believe in the tales? He pulled his hood tighter against his face. "Yes," he said.

In the city, the storm hit. Dust tornados erupted between canvas pavilions and scattered citizens; people hobbled to shelter and closed flap tents behind themselves. Wind bit at Simon's hood, growling, trying to yank it from his face. He ducked under a rope and crawled beneath a canvas wall to escape.

"Come closer," announced a voice.

He was in a tent behind a crowd of bent figures. Oil lamps tarnished their own light with sticky fog, but Simon could make out red and gold-painted letters on a banner sagging wearily from the ceiling: "Scientific Marvels."

"Come closer," said the voice again. "This is only a sample of the wonder awaiting you beyond the ticket door."

The mass pushed forward and splintered. Through a gap of people, Simon spotted the announcer. He was thin and graceful, waving a magician's wand toward a passage at the front. He adjusted a red visor over his eye with his palm—his left hand had no fingers at all—and called out to his customers again. "Five dollar equivalent, folks, just five, to see the most amazing evidence science has to offer!"

A stout woman held out a jar beside the man. People began funneling past her, dropping their barter into her jar before disappearing through a beaded curtain into the next room.

"Grotesque monsters of a past age," called the announcer. "Aberrations of nature! See the truth our government doesn't want you to know!"

Simon reached the woman and dropped a nail into her jar. She batted her eye and smiled. Beads clattered against his chest, then parted.

More oil lamps spit greasy light into the next room. Acrylic boxes glittered atop wooden crates, and Simon had to peer closely to look inside them. In one, a skeletal hand splayed its fingers. In another, a thick bone dangled from a string.

He was making his way toward a case that contained something skull-shaped, when the announcer appeared in the corner of the room beneath a blinding spotlight. "Gawk, my friends! Here you will find no plaster, no wax. These artifacts are genuine!"

"Rubbish," said a lumpy man in faded overalls.

"Where's the amazing part?" called a woman.

"You took my five for this?"

The announcer waved his hand. "Not this," he said. "What you are about to witness will change your perception of the truth forever!"

The stout woman slapped a drum roll onto a set of rotting bongos.

"Get on with it," someone muttered.

The announcer hitched his wrists around something in the shadows beside him. He grunted and pulled. A wheeled cage, covered with gold lamé, squeaked into view beneath the spotlight. The drum roll stopped. The announcer yanked the fabric. The crowd collectively gasped. Even Simon.

Inside the cage, with long, creamy fingers gripping the bars, and two brown eyes staring vacantly toward her bare feet, squatted the most beautiful woman Simon had ever seen.

Someone screamed.

"Cover it up!" yelled another.

Then laughter started, screeching like crows, stinging Simon's ears. Pebbles were thrown, bouncing off the bars and her smooth arms. She reacted then, squeezing into the corner of her cage and covering her head with her hands. The sagging flower-print fabric tied around her neck and waist left her ribs and thighs exposed to the sting of the rocks, and she whimpered, twitching with each concussion.

"Stop!" Simon clawed his way through the crowd and threw himself against the cage. Stones pelted his spine.

"Get back!" The announcer cried. He tugged at Simon's arm, but the rain of pebbles forced him away. "Don't damage the specimen," he called into the hysteria, waving his arms.

"Don't be afraid," said Simon. The woman didn't react, until he reached his hand toward her shoulder. She snapped her teeth at his fingers, catching the frayed end of his gauze. When he pulled back his hand, the gauze unwrapped, dangling from her lips.

Simon quickly tucked his hand into his armpit, but not before she noticed it. Her eyes darted toward his covered face.

"He's got a hand like the freak!"

The crowd surged forward. He felt knobby fingers pinching. He heard the rip of his cloak. He tasted acid at the back of his throat.

Then a tent support groaned, and another, and another. The wood poles arched inward, and the people stopped yelling, stopped pulling. All went still, until a twist of wind, sand-stung and howling, slammed against the roof. Support poles shattered. Canvas collapsed.

Simon felt the cage tip over, dragging him with it, as the tent fell to the storm. More screams came, and bodies writhed, panicking. He heard a pop of flame. An oil lamp caught fire beside him. He tried to roll, but he was entombed in canvas, unable to navigate.

"Get out," someone whispered near his ear, and in an instant, he recognized the voice of the sled driver. "Now's your chance," he said.

"I want the girl," said Simon, feeling through the bars beneath him. He touched flesh that retreated. There was a grunt of metal, and then a soft hand enwrapped his fingers. "Let's go," he said to the driver, somehow recognizing the woman's touch.

He heard the slice of a knife through fabric and felt a blast of hot wind. He lifted his face. The desert squall dulled the sun, but he knew it was there, somewhere beyond the great, dizzying swirl, and he crawled toward it. Beside him, the sled driver struggled on hands and knees. Behind him, the woman wrestled to freedom still holding his hand.

They thumped almost simultaneously into a new

wall. Simon patted this third tent, searching for an opening. Something gave way, and he toppled—they toppled—headfirst into quiet. The storm snarled outside while they all caught their breath.

Finally the man got to his feet. He stared down at Simon, his eye narrowed, his lips pursed. Simon knew he'd lost his hood between there and here, but he just met the man's gaze with his double eyes. The woman rolled to her side and stared, too. She touched Simon's rounded nose.

"You two should come with me," said the driver.

"I don't want—"

"I don't intend to give you any." He gave Simon a hand up.

The moment Simon stood, he stiffened. Before him were rows of acrylic cases, stretching from one end of the tent to the other.

"Don't look," said the man. "Just follow me." He led them through the center aisle between boxes.

But Simon looked. To his left, a clear container bubbled with bile-colored fluid. A foot wobbled about in the liquid, but not a bony, ancient artifact. It was a fleshy foot with five toes, skin furrowed and unraveling where it had been hacked from an ankle. To his right, a hand leaked discolored foam into its watery container, bubbles knocking into jointed fingers, massaging it into a gruesome wave.

"Don't look," Simon said to the woman behind him, and he urged her closer to wrap his arm around her waist.

"She can't hear you," said the driver.

Simon tried to keep his gaze on the man's back, but a glance at other boxes showed him a gristled knee joint. A pair of eyeballs. A length of intestine.

"My God," said Simon. "Is this—?"

"No," said the man. "This is not what you've been searching for." He ducked through the tent flap.

Outside, storm twisters were dissipating. Smoke from the collapsed canvas behind them was thinning. Other pavilions were beginning to rustle with activity. "Hurry," said the man, and urged them on.

They passed tents, and more tents, into the heart of the old city. The woman gaped at the clearing sky, breathed deeply of the grimy air.

"Where are we going?" asked Simon.

The man paused at a steel door hinged into brick rubble. "To meet your others." He tapped a combination onto a number pad beside the door, and it lurched open.

"Others?"

The man led them inside to windowless dark, closed the door behind. "There are many now. More than ever. They find us, or we find them."

He dragged a heavy grate from a hole in the concrete floor and snapped on a penlight. A metal ladder clung to the side of the hole and disappeared into shadow.

Simon exchanged a look with the woman. She smiled. Then she shimmied into the hole and descended.

"What's down there?" Simon asked the man.

"A hospital. A laboratory. A home."

"Whose home?"

"Yours, if you like. We'll study you, but we'll take care of you, too."

Simon grimaced, glanced where the tent of body parts would be on the other side of the wall.

"That wasn't us," said the man. "We won't harm you. We believe you to be our future."

Simon studied the man, tried to find the truth behind his twisted face.

"You will always be free to leave," said the man. "So far, no one has wanted to."

"There are more like me? Like the woman? Down there?"

"Down there. And in San Antonio. And Seattle. We keep the secret, for now, until we better understand. Until they" —he gestured toward the door— "better understand."

Simon drew in a tense breath. He rubbed his hands over his weary face.

"You did tell me you were searching," said the man.

He did. He was. He peered again into the hole in the floor.

"You have found it," he said.

Simon nodded, and the sled driver stuck out his hand for a shake. Instead, Simon bent, dug the pebble from his shoe, and set it on the man's palm.

The man closed his eye and smiled, enclosed his fist around the stone. Then he opened his eye again and swept his arm over the hole.

"Welcome," said the man. "To the Freak Museum."

Ironwork Falcon

Doren knew machines. He didn't so much build clockwork items as grew them; oiled gears, springs, and scraps created themselves into being with the sculptor's touch of Doren's hands. He'd been born for it, or so his family and friends said. And his dwarven master, Grel.

It was a rare thing for a human to be apprenticed to another race, let alone a dwarf. Doren was the only one in generations to be honored by such a choice.

Which is why his twin brother, Efram, was such an embarrassment. Efram was as inept with metal as Doren was gifted. His brother did try; he often picked up tools in the barn they'd turned into a workshop, put items into the vise, or hammered metal scraps on the anvil, but usually he ended up just getting in the way. Until recently.

Lately, Efram only watched from a distance.

This afternoon, Doren knelt before his kiln, feeding logs into its stone maw and feeling its heat as a stinging rash over his face and chest. He heard Efram's quiet footsteps come to a halt behind him.

"Throw me the splintered one?" he asked, turning to open his arms for the catch.

Efram stood in the barn's stone entryway, backlit by the fierce July sun. His shoulders drooped and his hands were in the pockets of his canvas trousers. One leather suspender held its place over the shoulder of his frayed tunic; the other sagged against his hip.

"The stump right beside your foot," said Doren, still waiting.

His brother finally roused to movement. He bent and gave a grunt as he lifted the heavy oak stub against his chest. But rather than tossing it, he carried it to Doren and set it into his hands. "It's not hot enough."

"It's as hot as the stone can handle," Doren said. He shoved the log into the growing blaze, and pushed the kiln's door closed with a pair of snips.

"I know," said Efram. "But it's not enough."

"It's enough." Doren stood, backing one step from the kiln. The barn had already been suffocating when Doren came in to work. Now the place began to take on a heat that choked Doren's throat and sponged breath from his lungs. He removed his tunic and mopped at his face, but it didn't help. The fire only growled toward his skin, trying to roast it.

"You need coal," said Efram.

"I don't have any."

"The blacksmith—"

"Hendridge won't sell me any more until we pay back what's already on our credit." Doren dropped his tunic onto the dusty floor and dragged his charred cast-off table into a patch of afternoon sun. "Same with the traders, the farmers, and even Mrs. Farran."

The old biddy had been bringing pies and bread to their father in the months since their mother died. Then she began to bring her daughter, Mim, too, who smiled up at Doren with white teeth and bright eyes, offering her own sweet-smelling bread and gooseberry jam. When their father took sick, Mrs. Farran came less often. When their credit became stretched, Mim Farran stopped visiting altogether.

That's what made Doren such an embarrassment to himself. Being a gifted apprentice to a metalworking dwarf still didn't bring any work, when there was no work to be had. The hunting community had been struck with an illness that, at first, simply dwindled local prey. But then it took their trained hunting birds. Then it started taking the people who relied on them.

Doren wasn't convinced illness was killing his people as much as starvation and hopelessness, but sometimes it was hard to tell the difference.

"I've begged and borrowed as much as I'm going to," said Doren. "For now, this is where I am. Burning scavenged wood and hammering metal until either the illness gets me, too, or I finally outsmart it."

"With your bird, you mean." Efram stood back,

glaring at either the kiln or Doren, Doren couldn't quite tell.

"It can work, Eff." Doren hoisted a coiled slab of iron from against the stable wall and thudded it to his table. "Grel told me of a falconer in Brennege that used an eagle to catch a wolf. A wolf!" He looked over his shoulder at his brother. "Can you imagine a bird with the strength of an eagle and the size of a peregrine? Unstoppable. And made of clockwork? Can't get sick and die."

"An iron bird can't fly," said Efram. "Let alone hunt."

Doren clenched his jaw. "Mine will. When I'm finished, it will be as light as copper and strong as a bear."

"Not even you can pound iron into copper." Efram pointed at the kiln. "Definitely not with a fire that weak."

Weak? Doren's back felt like scorched leather and sweat was falling from his face and pooling on the table below. But he did know the difference between a wood fire and a coal fire. Coal burned hotter, which made the metal softer and less likely to crack when struck by a smith's hammer. "Then talent will have to make up for it," he said.

When Efram didn't reply, Doren decided he'd finally won the sporting match of the day. But he looked up to find Efram leaving as silently as he'd entered. "Talent!" he shouted after his brother. "Something you don't know much about!"

Efram's steps faltered at that. He cast a dark look over his shoulder. Then he altered his course; instead of heading into the stone cottage where their father lay dying, he turned toward the path to the woods.

Doren considered going after him, but what good would it do? He slid his fingers into his suede working gloves, and channeled his frustrations into his work.

Days passed in heat and sweat and dehydrated delirium. Doren had spent countless hours at his task, but was no nearer to a solution than before. The ironwork falcon's inner springs, gears, and steam-powered cylinders chimed and whirred with precision, but its outer casing, with iron-feathered wings, could not lift. Doren had pounded and hammered and trimmed and shaped, but his machine, and his salvation, was as grounded as stone.

Efram had become scarce. At least he stayed out of Doren's way, but apart from their father always being dressed in clean bedclothes, and their dishes left washed and dried every morning, Efram left no trace that he lived with them.

Leave it to his brother, younger by mere minutes, to dally like a schoolchild in the woods while Doren shouldered the burden of responsibility.

As dawn breathed gray fog, Doren was just piling up the last log of a freshly chopped woodpile. He'd risen early to stoke a hot kiln ahead of the afternoon sun, but the air was already thick and wet, and heavy as a wool cloak. Or maybe that was just his sense of looming failure.

He caught sight of Efram, scuttling from the tool shed behind the house to disappear into the oak and maple arms of the forest.

Doren was suddenly angry. If Efram couldn't be bothered to help smithing, he could at least lend his arms to stack wood and keep the kiln fire hot. He followed after him, stomping across the meadow.

But Efram was more agile in the woods than he, and when Doren reached the trees, he had difficulty tracking. Burrs caught on his trousers, branches slapped his heat-worn cheeks. Sometimes he heard footsteps in the underbrush, only to find a rabbit or a squirrel dashing off out of sight. He was just considering turning around, when he heard a new sound. He paused to listen.

Voices. Efram spoke quietly in the distance. There was a second voice Doren didn't recognize.

He crept carefully, now more curious than annoyed. He hunkered, hoping low-growing bracken and berry vines would camouflage him. Then, when he was close enough, he parted the leaves an elder bush to spy through them.

Efram was easy to spot in a small clearing. He spoke words Doren didn't understand and waved his hands toward a pile of kindling near where Doren was watching. At first, Doren smiled at the sight of his oafish brother making awkward, dancelike movements, until he realized Efram didn't look awkward at all. His fingers splayed, and his arms lifted and lowered with a kind of grace. Efram's neck elongated, his wide shoulders straightened. His voice took on a resonance, and, for just a moment, Doren wondered if it was even Efram he was watching after all.

Then the kindling lifted into the air, crashed into each other with the empty thud of a wooden windchime, and burst into an explosion of white light and heat.

The force threw Doren against the ground, knocking his breath from his lungs. His ears buzzed.

He lay there, stunned. Then, worried. "Efram?" he tried to call. He sat up, his wits slowly regathering. "Efram!" he shouted. He jumped to his feet and lunged into the clearing.

Efram stepped back, white-faced and startled. "Doren?"

Beside Efram, a slender maple tree pulled its branches into itself, cracking and splintering. The sound echoed across the forest, and Doren thought, just briefly, that he felt all the trees shudder in pain. Then the sound turned quiet and muffled. The tree-shape became man-shaped, wearing robes with long roots that shrank up into a bottom hem. When the man stepped forward, Doren could see his dark eyes and slender features, and that his skin was the silvery brown of maple bark.

A forest elf. He should have known. Doren could feel his upper lip curl in disgust.

The elf opened his arms. "Welcome, brother of

Efram."

"Go back to the ground that belched you out," Doren snarled, stepping forward. Then he grabbed Efram's elbow and yanked him nearly off his feet.

"Let go, Doren!" Efram said.

"Back home, Eff. Now. Father would soil his bed if he knew you were here with one of them."

"Father does know I'm here!" Efram tightened his arm and broke Doren's grip. "You're not the only one who can apprentice, you know. You have no claim to all the family's talent."

Doren stopped short. "Father knows?"

"He sees them as I do," said Efram. His brother moved to stand beside the elf, and he took the elf's hand. The elf smiled at Efram, tenderly. Personally. Efram gave the elf's hand a reassuring squeeze.

"No!" Doren lurched toward them. He gave Efram a push, separating the two. "How dare you?" Then he turned his fury to the elf. "How dare *you?* You killed our mother! You're killing our father! You don't get to have my brother, too."

But then Efram pushed at him from behind, and Doren stumbled. As he caught his footing, Efram stepped between him and the elf.

Efram's eyes narrowed at Doren. He lowered his chin, met Doren's anger with his own. "Master Grel taught you lies."

"Someone is lying to you Eff, but it isn't me or my master," said Doren. He spoke to his brother, but he was glaring at the elf.

The elf didn't move, didn't speak. He just looked back at Doren with a gaze that was calm, steady.

It turned Doren's anger hard and sharp. "Your magic has defiled the woods," said Doren. "Infected our birds. Our people are starving and dying because of you."

"No," said the elf, then. His voice was the sound of a strong wind through the grasses of high summer. "It is your master's people who dig into Earth's viscera. Your master's people and you." He raised his chin and looked down at Doren, seeming taller than he was. "You tunnel into her, grinding at her, stealing parts from her. You don't even cover the wounds you create. You weaken her. Sicken her."

"You accuse *me,* now?" Doren said, his hands balling into fists.

"Stop!" said Efram. He held up his hands and looked over his shoulder at the elf. "Laevi, please." Then, he looked back at Doren. "Brother," he said. He didn't often refer to Doren that way, so when he did, it gave Doren pause.

"I don't ask you to agree with Laevi, any more than you would insist I agree with Master Grel. You go on with your training," said Efram. He lowered his hands to his sides. "And I'll go on with mine."

The elf's hand, like a willow branch, settled onto Efram's shoulder.

"Ha!" Doren didn't have to stand here and defend his master or himself. He stepped back. "Play with the trees all you want, Eff. When you're the next one starving to death, try eating their poison."

Doren turned and plunged through the trees, back toward his barn and his metals, toward the things he could grasp in his hand and feel with fingers. The things of earth that were solid and real, that he could see working, and could understand.

Although he had only a vague idea of how to get back, he would rather walk for a few extra hours than admit he might get lost on the way.

In the night, he heard his father cry out. He scrambled from bed, blind in the darkness, and stumbled down the hallway to his father's room. Efram was already there, lighting a tallow candle and speaking in soothing tones.

"There now," he said. He knelt, taking Father's hand. "I'm here."

"My boys," said Father, his voice dry and distant. "My boys."

"Don't give up," said Efram. "Doren works night and day. Soon his ironwork falcon will fly, and I know you'll want to see it when it does."

"Yes." Father smiled faintly, his eyes still closed. "He is a gift."

"Yes," said Efram. He turned his face toward Doren, his dark eyes rimmed with moisture. "He is."

Tears threatened Doren, too. The fatigue and disappointment of the past weeks rushed in all at once to overwhelm him. He braced against the wooden doorframe.

"And so are you," said Father, reaching for Efram's hand.

Doren pushed away from the doorframe, just managing to reach the side of the bed before he collapsed to his knees. He took Father's other hand, seeing his brow twitch, and his wrinkled throat move with a dry swallow. Doren looked over at Efram, then. The two of them, both holding their father's hands, like when they were children.

Efram looked at Doren, too, and in that moment, they both shared the other's fear. Just like when they were children.

"My boys," said Father.

Doren awoke with a stiff neck and swollen eyes. He lifted his head, orienting. He'd fallen asleep on his knees beside his father's bed, clasping his father's hand. For a moment, he startled at the peaceful look on his father's face, but realized his hand was warm. Father was breathing.

He rose slowly, working out kinks in his back and legs. Then he began to walk toward the galley kitchen, but paused at the sounds coming from the barn. Efram was in his workshop.

He crossed the dawn-weary meadow toward the barn, and leaned into the entryway. "Taking up my tools?" he asked.

Efram startled, and spun, eyeing his brother sheepishly. "Not your tools. Your kiln."

"What?"

"I've been practicing a spell," Efram said. "One Laevi taught me."

"A spell," Doren repeated.

"To make heat that can soften metal without burning skin," said Efram.

Doren frowned. "Heating metal without wood? Without coal?"

"A little wood," said Efram. "But no coal. I'm not very good at it yet, but I will be." He squared his shoulders.

"I don't want any magic in my falcon," said Doren.

"No," said Efram, shaking his head. "That's all you. I only want to give you a fire."

Doren looked at the kiln. It sat empty, all the wood from the previous fire burned down into useless ash. "All right, let's see if you can do it," he said, straightening off of the doorframe.

Efram smiled, his eyes bright. "Yeah?"

"Sure," Doren decided aloud, mostly because he didn't think it was possible.

Then Efram began slowly circling the kiln, quietly speaking those strange words.

Doren pulled his charred table closer and started to lay out his tools, just in case it *was* possible.

◊

Behind them, their father stood weakly in the doorframe, unseen, and watching them. Smiling.

"My boys," he said.

Elvis Landing

I'd eaten dinner alone again. Gene forgetting our anniversary wasn't so surprising as my hoping he'd remember it. I'd actually bought a new dress at Savmart, and splurged on a box of Fashion Highlights that was supposed to "unleash the power of red" in my otherwise ash-brown hair.

Those highlights reflected in the kitchen window as I stood at the sink and scraped cheesy grits into the garbage disposal.

The screen door rattled. "Jenay Porter! Let me in. Girl, I got news."

It was my neighbor, Auburn. I finished scraping cold grits into the garbage disposal, and then wiped my damp hands on my apron. I smiled at her through the mesh while I tugged open the metal hook and eye latch.

Her brown face was damp around the edges where it met her black, braided hair. "Must be some news for you to walk all this way in mosquito twilight."

"Oh, it is." She poked a rolled newspaper toward my nose. "American Idol is coming to Memphis."

I laughed. "Well, good luck. Tell Simon I said hi." I turned to walk the six feet to the sink and finish washing my dishes.

Auburn snatched at my elbow. "Tell him yourself. Come on, Jenay, I heard you sing, and I know church choir ain't enough for you."

I shook my head. "I'm ten years and twenty pounds away from the kind of idol they're looking for."

"You open your mouth, they won't see nothing but a shining star."

I smiled at Auburn. She was the closest thing I had to a best friend, and the closest thing I had to a neighbor, living out here in Eads County, Tennessee. City spread was creeping toward us, but it wasn't in any hurry. My husband, Gene, said someday contractors would pay us good money for our six acres, and it would be our ticket out. But what good was a ticket when I had nowhere to go?

Auburn peered closer at me then. "You got a new apron?"

"A dress. It was on sale."

"And you got yourself some highlights!"

I touched my hair. "Too much stripe, maybe?"

"Naw, you look good!" Her brown eyes caught the flicker of the dinner candle still melting on the kitchen table. Gene and I had paid ten dollars for that table at a garage sale. Candlelight only brought out its deep, varnished ugliness. "Special night?" Auburn asked.

"Anniversary."

"So how come I don't see no Gene Porter, aka husband?"

I plunged my hands into dishwater and scrubbed at an iced tea glass.

"You know that man is no good. You got to change those locks, girl."

"He's a good man. He's just…"

"He's just dying a slow death and strangling you along with him." Auburn set the newspaper on the counter and dragged over a plastic chair. She sat, folding her thin arms. Her fuchsia sundress wilted across her legs and dangled against my linoleum floor. "All your working at Pancake Hut, and you just hand the money to him. Don't think I don't know what's going on."

I didn't want to talk about this. Not tonight. "I know you mean well, Auburn—"

"But you're not going to listen."

"It's just complicated."

"What's complicated about showing a man the bottom of your boot next time he comes home strung out and smelling like a kind of perfume you don't have in your bathroom?"

I stacked a dried plate into the cupboard. "He didn't used to be like this."

"Shoot…none of them are what they used to be." Auburn stood, leaned over the table, and blew out the candle. "I'll bet if tonight was that horse's birthday, he'd have been here with a store-bought cake."

I gave her a look. She crossed her arms and gave it right back.

Sad thing was, she was right. Gene loved Paddycake, the sway-backed old Morgan mare in our tiny barn. She was a gentle soul, and I could like her, myself, if Gene hadn't spent more money on feed and tackle for her in the last year than he'd ever spent on all my anniversary presents put together.

I stared out the kitchen window into the dwindling daylight, trying to figure out how my life had come to this. I didn't often do that, but now and again, when I was particularly tired or sad, I'd indulge myself. "Auburn?"

She came to stand beside me at the sink.

I looked at our reflections in the window; hers dark, mine light. "How long you think it is we have to suffer for all our mistakes?"

She shook her head. "Only God knows."

"You think he adds up all the sinning into one big dark hole, and makes you pay all at once? Or that he gives out punishment in small, quiet ways that last a while, the way we did the sinning to begin with?"

She put her hand on my arm. "Maybe you're so busy punishing yourself God doesn't have to."

Just then a loud whistle broke out across the trees, and I peered through the window. "Do you hear that?"

"Someone shoot off a bottle rocket?" asked Auburn.

"People know not to come on our property." I

pulled off my apron and pushed open the screen door to go investigate. The door slammed hard when Auburn came out, too. We rounded the corner of the house, scuffing through a dirt patch where grubs had killed the grass.

The whistle turned to a screech, and I slapped my hands over my ears. The ground rumbled through my shoes and into my legs, like when Gene ran the tractor too close to the house. "What is going on?" I shouted over the noise.

"Something's coming!" Auburn pointed to the gray sky.

Clouds swirled into a funnel, then spat out something dark. Something dark and long and turning end over end, heading straight for us. "Look out!" I said, and reached for Auburn, but in the time it took to duck, the explosion was all around us.

We were thrown to the ground. Something hit the back of my head. I heard a whinnying scream. I lay stunned, my left arm wrenched against the side of the house, and my right wrapping Auburn's shoulders. Everything went silent again, except for a droning hum coming from somewhere behind us.

I rolled to my back. I sat up. I stared. There, where our tiny barn used to be, was a pile of wood rubble. In the center of the rubble, slammed so hard the ground had caved to a crater, was a black cylinder the size of a Chevy truck. My eyes searched for signs of movement. There were none. Poor Paddycake.

"Hoo, girl," said Auburn, where she sat cross-legged on the ground, shaking her head. "You know Gene is going to find a way to make this your fault."

Gene had never hit me, but if there was ever going to be a first time, this was probably it. "Maybe Paddy's all right," I said.

"She's fine, if you like your steaks well done." Auburn pushed to her feet and swiped her dirtied palms across her skirt.

"We ought to be able to sue somebody," I said. "I've heard of jet engines falling off and smashing houses. People sue for that."

She shrugged. "Should we call 911 or something?"

I tried to stand, too, but nausea gripped me, and a headache rushed in to pound at my brain. I stayed seated. "You go call. I don't feel good."

"You don't look so good. And you're bleeding." She pressed her hand to the back of my head.

The hum coming from the barn suddenly stopped. We both turned to look. A strip of light ran up the side of the thing and around it, splitting it in two. Another band of light crossed over the top. "Are you seeing what I'm seeing?" asked Auburn.

"I've got a head wound. I could be hallucinating."

"If what you're seeing is some kind of U.F.O., we're both hallucinating."

The upper section peeled open like a boiled peanut. "Holy crap," said Auburn.

I couldn't speak. I could only watch in disbelief as two arms reached out of the top and scrabbled for hold along the smooth sides.

"We should run now," said Auburn.

I nodded.

A domed head appeared next, but in the failing light I couldn't see details. Then an entire shape—the size of a child—crawled over the side and dropped hard to the ground. The figure laid still.

"Forget 911," said Auburn. "I'm calling a newspaper." She ran into the house.

I was alone, bleeding, and sharing the darkness with a crashed U.F.O. and its creepy pilot. Well, I assumed it was creepy. Aliens usually were.

Of all the ways I'd imagined spending my wedding anniversary, this wasn't one of them. I was struck with the most consuming, overwhelming sense of helplessness. I couldn't think. I couldn't even grasp what was really happening. My head hurt, the barn was gone, and right where I was sitting felt like a perfect place to take a nap. I laid back and closed my eyes.

Moments later, I was nudged. Hot breath blew across my face. Strong hands rolled me to my side. I felt fingers slide into my hair, which stung my scalp, and then my headache faded. I opened my eyes to find a young man with blonde hair smiling down at me.

"Get back!" Auburn pointed Gene's shotgun toward the man. He yelped and fell, trying to wave his hands and scoot backward at the same time.

"It's okay, Auburn," I said, and scrambled around to get to my feet. "He helped me. I think."

"You just get back, you freak!" She leveled the weapon at his nose.

"Besides, look at him. He's not even an alien." The man stared up at Auburn, his eyes hazel and wide. His skin was pale, but he had as human a face as any I'd seen. He wore a brown t-shirt with faded jeans and bowling shoes like he'd just walked out of a men's store catalogue.

Auburn narrowed her eyes. She looked from the man to the barn and back. "Well, if he's not the alien that climbed out of the U.F.O., where did it go? And where did this guy come from?"

"You'd better tell her who you are," I said to the man. "She might really shoot."

He didn't answer.

"Seriously," I said.

He looked from me to Auburn. "Seriously," he said.

Auburn arched her brows. "Are you mocking my friend?"

"Seriously," he said.

"Why, I ought to—"

"Wait, Auburn." I stepped between the man and the gun. "We're all confused right now. Let's just think." I reached down to help the man stand. When he did, I had to look up into his face, just a little. A nice face. I might have thought he was a college kid, but his eyes looked older. Wiser, somehow. "Did you come out of that spaceship?" I asked him, wondering if a sane person should ask such a question.

He looked toward the barn. "Yes."

"Holy crap," said Auburn. "What do we do with him?"

"Did you call the newspaper?"

"They hung up on me." She lowered the tip of the shotgun to the ground. "Think we should try 911?"

"I don't know. I don't know what to do."

"I mean no harm," he said, and held out his hands.

Auburn snorted. "Next he'll be asking us to take him to our leader."

"Well, maybe we should."

"We need to send him on his way, is what we need." Auburn turned for the house. "Make him go bother someone else. We'll tell Gene the barn blew a gas main, or something."

"The barn doesn't have a gas main."

The man followed after Auburn, and I reached to stop him, but he broke my grip and kept going. He climbed the steps of the porch, looked around himself in the doorway, and went through.

Inside, Auburn opened the fridge and popped the top off a beer. When I flipped on the kitchen light switch, the man startled. Then he smiled, and I could swear he looked embarrassed.

"Are you thirsty? Hungry?" I asked. If I didn't know what else to do, I could at least feed him. It always worked for my grandma.

"Yes," he said.

"You like grits?"

"Yes."

I offered him the plate of dinner I'd been saving for Gene. He poked his finger into the white lump of hominy and then licked it. Then he licked the grits, trying to get them into his mouth.

"Here, try this." I gave him a spoon. And I led him to the table to sit.

"Shoot. Any alien who likes grits can't be all bad," said Auburn. She sipped her beer, and turned her head lopsided to stare at him. "He's cute. Doesn't seem so scary, up close."

"Not all bad," said the man, and wiped his greasy hands down his thighs.

"So...ah. Did you fix my head? My headache?" I touched at the base of my skull where I'd been bleeding.

"Yes," he said.

"Can you fix other things? Like my barn? The horse?"

"Ain't no one can fix that horse, Jenay," said Auburn.

"Well maybe he can!"

"Horse?" he asked.

I slid Auburn's newspaper off the counter and pressed it open on the table. I flipped pages, searching for a picture to explain. "Maybe he can get everything put back before Gene gets home."

"How's he supposed to do that?"

"Well, I don't know, but he must have powers or something. He's from another planet, isn't he?"

Auburn laughed. "Yeah, and he can't even steer his ship right, let alone muster some kind of magical..."

As she spoke, his hand touched a sales flyer in the newspaper for Burger Barn. Instantly, his hair lengthened and turned brown, his t-shirt grew a collar, and a Burger Barn cap sprouted on his head. He transformed into the model in the advertisement. "Burgers like dad used to make," he said, and smiled.

Auburn's mouth fell open. Mine did too.

"You got a TV Guide?" she asked.

"What?"

"A TV Guide." She whirled around and ran into the living room. She dove at piles of magazines on the floor, rummaged through stacks of old newspapers. "Got to be a picture of Denzel in here somewhere."

"Auburn…"

"That alien just might get him some extraterrestrial booty before he—"

"Auburn!"

She returned to the kitchen with an armload of papers. "Tell me you ain't thinking it." She pushed the candle out of the way and dropped magazines, newspapers, and VCR covers onto the table.

"How do you even know he has the right…well, the right…?"

She put her hand on her hip. "Well, look at him. Except I liked him better before. We got to get him out of that nasty uniform." She thumbed through *Country Music Magazine.*

"Just because he looks like a man doesn't mean he is one. He can probably change into anything."

"Yeah," she said, and frowned. "Let's see." She flipped to an interview in the magazine with Dolly Parton and spun her picture to face him.

He narrowed his eyes.

"Well, go on," said Auburn. "Touch it."

He rested his fingertips on the photograph. Nothing happened. "I am man," he said.

"Ha!" said Auburn. "I told you."

"Well, it doesn't matter," I said, and pushed all the papers to the far side of the table. "Whatever he is, he didn't come thousands of miles to sleep with an earth girl. He was on his way to somewhere else."

"Somewhere else," he said, and stood.

"And we have to figure out how to get him back on his way."

Auburn quirked her mouth. "You going to take him to Sav-mart for machine parts?"

"Maybe." I cleared his plate from the table and walked to the sink. "But he can't stay here tonight. You'll have to take him home, Auburn. We'll figure out what to do tomorrow."

"Me? Why I got to be seen with a kid who works at Burger Barn?" She reached for a magazine. "There must be someone dark and hunky in one of these."

The sound of squealing tires made me drop the plate into the sink. It splashed, dotting the window and my cheeks with soapy water. "Oh no," I said, spinning around to stare at the door. "That's Gene! Quick, take him into the other room."

I rounded the end of the counter and pushed the man toward the living room. Auburn jostled and dropped her magazine. "Your back door broken?"

"Painted shut. Just give me a few minutes to get Gene into the bedroom, then you two sneak out. I'll come over first thing when Gene leaves for work."

"Hiding out like a criminal," I heard Auburn say as I hurried to the door.

"Criminal," said the Burger Barn alien.

"Honey, I'm home!" Gene shouted, waving a paper bag, stumbling up the walk. The porch light turned his moustache to spider legs, lit the bags beneath his eyes. Moths dive-bombed around his head, making him look like a cartoon character that'd been beaned with an anvil.

"Hey," I said, and swung open the door. "Hurry, don't let in the bugs."

He swayed past me and tossed the paper bag on the counter. Then he slowly spun, his eyes glazed, taking in the table, the sink of water. "Hell... I missed dinner. Cleaned it right up, didn't you?" He grabbed my hips and pressed against me. "It's okay, I got me a little dessert." He laughed, gave me a push, and grasped the paper bag again. "A little macaroni and cheese. Yeah."

I stiffened. "You know I don't like you to bring that home."

"'Course I brought it home." He kissed my cheek, his mouth smelling of whisky. "Happy Anniversary, sweets." He pressed the bag into my hand.

I recoiled. "Gene—"

"Didn't think I remembered, did you?" He pulled at my arm, tugging me toward the bedroom. "Come on. Old times sake. For when you used to love me."

Something crashed so loudly in the living room it startled us both.

"The hell?" Gene squinted his bleary eyes and looked toward the sound.

"Probably a stack of papers fell over. Come on." This time, I was tugging him. "You were saying something about old times."

"What the...?" He shoved me away and stomped toward the living room. "I'll kill him. You thought you could sneak someone in here and I'd be so hammered I wouldn't even know! On our anniversary! You cheating little—!"

"It's not what you think," I said, sounding stupid to even myself. I ran, following, trying to yank at him, make him stop.

And then he did stop. Suddenly. I bumped into his spine.

"You ain't nothin' but a hound dog," said Elvis Presley, standing next to Auburn, who was holding a *Country Music Magazine* in her trembling hands.

Elvis pushed up his black sunglasses. Moonlight shone through the curtains and sparkled the swirling rhinestones across his shoulders. Then he settled the sequined strap of his white guitar into place, and nodded. "Cryin' all the time."

"I'll be a sonuva..." Gene laughed. "I knew you weren't dead! Standing right here in my living room!" He stepped back and put his arm around my waist, his eyes brighter, his moustache twitching. "You'll sing for us?" He shifted his weight on his feet, tightened his grip around me. "Damned if this isn't the best anniversary present you could have thought up, Jenay."

I sent a look toward Auburn, who smiled. I tried to thank her with my eyes. She nodded.

"I'll sing," said Elvis.

"I'm a fool?" asked Gene.

Elvis closed his eyes. His fingers strummed. Then he opened his mouth and crooned as rich as any recording I'd ever heard.

If I'm a fool for loving you then that's just what I want to be...

They're saying I am just your clown and any fool could see... that you're just having fun and you're not in love with me.

The things they're saying may be true, but there's something they can't see. If I'm a fool for loving you... then that's just what I want to be.

Elvis kept playing, but he stopped singing and was looking strangely at Gene. I followed his gaze to find Gene crying. His face was pale. He lowered his chin. "You better lay me down, Jen."

I hooked my arm around his back and he leaned on me while we shuffled to the bedroom. We'd barely made it to the bed when he collapsed, twisted onto his side, and went still.

I knelt to slip off his shoes. I heard steps behind me and knew it was Auburn. "Thank you for that," I said.

"I was just trying to help you, I didn't mean to give him a present."

"But you did. It was nice."

I looked up to find her with her arms crossed, scowling at Gene. "No. I didn't want to give him a present."

She stared down at him, and I saw what she saw: sallow skin, haggard age around his closed eyes, a disintegrating nose. My tears welled.

I stood, pulled a cotton blanket over his legs, and kissed his earlobe. My foot crinkled the paper bag that had fallen onto the floor, so I picked it up.

I brushed past Auburn and came face to face with Elvis in the hallway. I stopped short. "That is really unnerving," I said.

He touched my cheek. "Cryin' all the time."

"I'm okay," I said.

He looked into the bedroom. He removed his sunglasses. He sniffed toward Gene like a Labrador and grimaced at the puddle of drool forming beneath Gene's cheek.

"He wasn't always like this," I said.

"Yeah, so you keep saying," said Auburn. She shook her head. Then she scuffed through the hallway and reached for the front door. "I'm going home to take some aspirin. You bring our buddy over, or don't, I don't know." She stepped out onto the porch, and then paused. "If you bring him, don't bring him looking like that."

The porch light lost track of her and she disappeared into the dark.

I walked to the sink. I opened the paper bag and removed a small plastic jeweler's bag filled with white powder. I turned it over in my hand. "It's my fault," I said.

Elvis set his sunglasses on the kitchen counter and leaned onto his elbows, watching me.

"The way Gene is, it's my fault." The words were harder to say than I thought they would be; they clotted in my throat. "He never touched the stuff before. He just drank a little beer on the weekends. He was a really good guy. Kind of straight-laced, I thought then. Went to church and everything."

The powder leered at me through the plastic bag. *Happy Anniversary*, it said to me. *Let's start a party.*

"He would drive up to Nashville to listen to me sing. I was in a band then. I was living the life. Making connections. Had a song played on the radio."

It felt so long ago, as though I'd dreamed it. But I'd spent so much time then being high, I might as well have dreamed it. Now and again, I wondered how much of it had been real.

"Gene took me to clinics, tried to help me get clean. Sometimes I was, for a while. But I'd sing, and I'd party, and I'd lose days, weeks." I felt the words spew from me like vomit, and I emotionally convulsed, unable to stop them. "And I would tease him. Call him names. The first time he snorted, I talked him into it. I *talked him into it.*"

I became aware of the plastic bag squeezed hard into my fist. When I uncurled my fingers, I saw the bag had broken, and white powder dusted my skin. *The only way to stay together is to share everything,* I'd said then.

The only way to stay together.

I plunged my hand, bag and all, into the water in the kitchen sink. I let it soak, trembling, wishing the soap could wash away the memories, too. Lift them like grease from my mind, carry them down the drain.

"You probably don't understand a word I'm saying," I said.

"Yes," came the answer, but with a voice that startled me. I spun. There stood Gene, his eyes bright and young, his hair curled under near his ears from needing a haircut. He wore a gray tie pulled loose at his blue collar.

"Gene?"

"Hey, beautiful."

I stared, my breath caught. Then I hugged my arms around his neck, pressed our cheeks together. "Is it really you?"

He enclosed his arms around my back. It was such a familiar embrace, so right. He smelled of Old Spice and Downy; the scent of the man I loved. "I've missed you."

"Do you love me, sweets?" he asked, and I felt the question rumble through his chest. It was an old game. I'd almost forgotten it.

"I love you a little."

"A little or a lot?" he asked.

"A little and a lot." I smiled, and leaned back to let him kiss me.

"Here?" His lips pressed against my throat.

"A little," I said.

"Here?" He kissed my chin.

"A little."

"Here?" He tasted the corner of my mouth.

I giggled, feeling silly. Feeling a bride. "A lot," I said.

"Show me." He grinned. Then he skulked backward into the bedroom, his brows mischievously quirked. I watched him until he closed the door, and then I straightened my dress and fluffed my hair.

I crept closer. I paused with my hand on the knob. "Gene?"

Then my eyes caught on the photograph in a rusty frame in the hallway. In the picture stood Gene, his eyes bright and young, his hair curled under near his ears from needing a haircut. He wore a gray tie pulled loose at his blue collar. It had been our first anniversary.

I lifted the picture from the wall and hugged it to me. And I cried.

I woke up on the floor of the hallway. I ached from where I'd fallen asleep with the picture frame pressed to my face.

Then Gene gave a shout that I heard all the way from the back yard and through the closed front door. The sound came from near the barn.

I scrambled to my feet, hurrying to find him. I lunged out the door and around the house. When I caught sight of the barn, I skidded to a stop. It was still a mangled mess, with a crater in the center instead of Paddycake, but the black cylinder was gone.

Gene was stomping his feet, throwing wood planks, and cursing so hard white foam clung to the corners of his mouth. "Do you see this?" he asked when I got closer, but I knew he didn't expect me to answer.

"What happened?"

"How the hell should I know?" He kicked at a plank. "Maybe I ought to ask you! You hated my horse."

"I didn't hate her," I said. "I wouldn't hurt her."

"Wouldn't you?" His eyes churned so dark I flinched. Then he drew up straight and blinked. He turned his back. "You wouldn't," he said. "I'm sorry. You wouldn't."

I inched forward and laid my hand against his shoulder blade. "Maybe it was aliens."

He laughed a bitter sort of sound. "Yeah." Then he sat on a rock and held his hands against his face.

"I'm sorry, Gene." I knelt beside him. "I know you loved Paddycake."

"I did," he said. "I loved that stupid animal." He lowered his hands. "But it's not just her, it's the barn. And it's not just the barn, it's you. And it's not just you, it's everything."

"What do you mean?"

"It's every day. Like something has swooped down, blown our life into tiny bits, and killed us. I mean, think about it." He stood up and held out his arms, eyes looking around at the rubble. "We're seeing this now, but it really happened a long time ago. Didn't it?"

I knelt for a while, watching him. Remembering him. Recognizing him in this moment between moments.

"What?" He lowered his arms.

I stood and went to him. "Do you love me, sweets?"

"What?"

I drew in a deep breath. "Do you love me, sweets?"

He regarded me, his brows pulling together.

"Do you—?"

"A little," he said.

I smiled. "A little or a lot?"

He smiled, too. Sad. Lost. "A little and a lot."

I took his hand. "Come show me.

The Last Girl

She walked slowly through the rubble of what was once a metropolis. Mountains of concrete were once roads, buildings. Cars rusted out wherever they'd stopped, seatbelts strapped around skeletons. Silt covered everything, blowing clouds from eerie corners.

She stared at the campfire she'd built at the steps of the old church. She cried as she walked toward it, carrying the body of her golden retriever. She tossed the body onto the fire, scattering sparks.

She watched her friend char and burn. She dropped to her knees. Going numb. Her rotting backpack slid from her shoulders and spilled out canned peaches, baked beans. The tie holding her makeshift spear in place came loose from a strap, and it rolled away, out of the circle of heat made by the flames.

Behind her, scrabbling noises came close, drawn by the smoke, no doubt. And the smell. She stayed near, making sure nothing could drag him off to be eaten. She also heard the strange, clicking vocal sounds. She always heard those sounds when she came to the city. She was too tired to care about them today.

Eventually, as the afternoon began to feel heavy and gray; the campfire faded, and her friend was ash and bone. She felt her soul burn with him. She was now just a shell.

She managed to push to her feet. She hadn't faced a night alone in a long time. She didn't want to. She picked up her backpack out of habit. She left her spear and her supplies where they'd fallen.

She walked away from the church, her backpack dragging from her hand, toward the block of stores missing shop windows and front doors. She kicked a stone, watched it skitter into a slab of broken asphalt. Then she stepped through the empty doorway of what used to be a drugstore.

She passed a newspaper rack where the papers were yellowed and curling. Headlines read **CAN HUMANS SURVIVE?** and **IS THIS THE END?** She'd forgotten how to read a long time ago, but some words, like those headlines, stayed bright and hot in her memory, and leaked into her dreams.

She walked to the makeup counter. She ran her fingers over dusty bottles of nail polish, and then tubes of lipstick. She opened a lipstick, peered in at the color. She also found eyeliner pencils; black, blue, green. She collected them.

She carried her things to a small mirror display and blew dust from the glass to see herself better. Then she opened the lipstick, wiped it across her mouth, and under her eyes. She unwrapped a black eyeliner pencil, and drew with that, too, in lines along her cheekbones, and in a great big X across each eye.

She searched out the highest mound of concrete rubble, a used-to-be building with so many floors it needed an elevator. It took the rest of the afternoon to pick her way to the top, and when she got there, she was breathless and bleeding from scratches.

She spotted a scrap of corrugated tin jutting out like a cliff, and when she eased onto it and looked down, she got dizzy in her stomach. It would be a long, long fall. She wondered if it would feel like flying. Maybe she would just land and feel nothing at all.

She outstretched her arms and closed her eyes. Pebbles came loose from beneath her feet, startling her. She tensed, opened her eyes to make sure she was still as far out on the ledge as she could go. She was.

Then she saw something. Color. A flower, growing from a crag filled with dirt in the rubble mountain. Yellow. She remembered yellow. Dandelions.

She inched back off the tin edge and got to her knees. She leaned down, reaching for the flower, fingers stretching.

Then, sounds of scrabbling. Those strange, clicking vocal noises. "You hear that, Dog?" she said. "Dog?"

She looked to her left were Dog should be, but he

wasn't. Her heart hurt again.

Something darted out from a heap of bricks in a flash of movement. It was gone again before she could suck in her breath, but she could hear rocks and concrete rattling, dislodged.

"Stay away from me, you freaks," she said, just like she'd heard her daddy say lots of times before. She realized she'd dropped her spear, so she picked up a broken brick and threw it where she heard noises. "Mutant freaks!" she yelled. Then she got to her feet and hurried as fast as she could back down through the skeleton of the building, to the ground.

She had to run, and keep running, trying to beat the darkness all the way back home.

Finally, she reached the smashed rail car where she kept all her things. Her hair stuck to her sweaty face, and her legs were cramping, but she made it just as the stars were beginning to blink. She pushed open the side-rolling door with a grunt, and then hoisted herself up and over the threshold.

She crawled toward the crate where she stored her candles in a big, metal bowl, all melted together with their wicks poking out. She felt under the crate for the lighter with the long neck and clicked it to flame. Then she tapped the flame to the wicks, lighting them into a bright torch.

Shadows flickered against the walls of the rail car, across her collection of weapons; sharp knives wrapped onto broom handles, a rusty hacksaw, a barbecue fork. Daddy taught her to protect herself and showed her how to make things from other things. He would be proud of her collection.

She only used the killing weapons when she was very, very hungry, though. She didn't like hurting rabbits or other fuzzy babies, and she hated the part where she had to pull off their skin. Sometimes their eyes popped out. Usually their insides smelled like poop. It was easier with Dog, because he could catch even squirrels, and he'd bring her things already dead.

He was a good boy. She missed him so much. She crawled over to the mound of blankets that was his bed, and laid her cheek on them, smelling him there, pretending he was there.

She must have fallen asleep, because she remembered dreaming that dog was moving around on his bed. She startled awake. The candlelight was gone, and moonlight streamed in, lighting the space brighter than even the candles.

She'd forgotten to close the door.

Something tickled her hand. She recoiled. She didn't like when bugs got on her skin or in her hair. Once, daddy cut off all her hair with his buzzy razor, just so the bugs wouldn't have anywhere to hide. Her hair was long again, though, and she didn't have a razor anymore.

But it wasn't a bug on her hand, it was a flower. Yellow.

Then she heard it again, that noise that woke her up. It was the sound Dog made when he got lost, or when he wanted a piece of food she took too long to share. But it wasn't right. It wasn't Dog.

She saw glowing eyes in a hunched shadow. She made a slow reach for her barbecue fork.

The shadow shifted, moved to the left.

She pointed her weapon and growled like Dog taught her to do.

The shadow wailed. It fell out of the rail car, made a bumping noise when it hit the ground. Girl crawled to the edge of the threshold and peeked over, but it was already gone.

Her heart was beating fast, and she felt like someone had punched her in the stomach. She caught her breath. Daddy would have been proud of her for defending herself, especially because she had remembered to keep moving when she was afraid. He used to tell her if she ever saw another person, to run. If she was trapped and couldn't run, use a killing weapon.

But then they stopped seeing other people anywhere. Instead, they kept seeing weird little shapes in the distance, and hearing throat noises and clicking sounds. Daddy told her they were mutant freaks who used killing weapons on all the other people until she and Daddy were the only two left. He said they ate all the people's skin and even the bones.

One night, Daddy had made her promise that when his time came, to make a big fire and put him in it, so mutant freaks couldn't eat his skin. He also made her promise to forgive him for not taking her with him. The next morning, Daddy never woke up.

She never got to ask him where he was going, and

why she couldn't go, too. But she kept her promises. Both of them. Sometimes, she got angry at Daddy whenever she thought about that morning, and she had to forgive him all over again.

It was happening now. She was angry. So, she took a deep breath, and said, "I forgive you, Daddy," and tried really, really hard to make it true.

Then she reached up for the handle of the rail car's door and slid it closed.

She slept too long the next morning. It was already hot and hazy by the time she pushed the door open and hopped down from the rail car. She hadn't thought much about what would happen the day after Dog. She'd lost her backpack somewhere, filled with food and water bottles. She was hungry and thirsty, so she would have to scrounge in the city for something to eat. It would take too long to hunt down a fuzzy baby.

While she walked, she sang the song she knew from when she still had Daddy. He taught it to her. She sang it to remember him, and now she would sing it to remember Dog.

"Aybee, Seedy, E, Eff, Gee... Age Eye Jay Kay Ellamennopee. Cubar ess, tee you me. Double you ask and why and see."

There was more, but she'd lost that, so she just sang the part she knew over and over, very loud and very sad, for Dog.

When she reached the edge of the city, she stopped singing and listened, instead. Just birds hopping around in nests built into the sides of broken things, and wind in the green trees sprouting up between cracks.

She thought she'd lost some food at the fire yesterday, but she didn't want to go there again so soon. She decided to try the food store where she'd found things in boxes in closets. She usually saved the store for emergencies. Today felt like one of those.

In the store, she passed dusty food boxes spilled across the floor from the last time she rummaged. Muffins were on the covers. "This tricked me once, Dog," she said. "I remember Daddy made muffins, so I thought this was muffins, but it isn't." She picked up a box and held it toward the light. "It tastes like sand and is not good for eating." She threw the box back onto the floor. She looked to her left to where Dog should be. He would have pounced the box and run off to play chase.

She walked around rubble, and ducked beneath broken, hanging pipes and wires to where a soot-covered cash register sat. She banged on the buttons, and it made a bell sound. She liked making the sound, but she still couldn't figure out how to make the drawer pop open. "There's probably just money in there, Dog. What good does that do me?"

She looked to her left where Dog should be. He would have tilted his head at the bell, his tongue hanging out.

Her stomach growled, and her tongue felt like paste. She could drink out of the bathroom faucet, although she didn't like to. The water was warm and tasted rusty. "But it's better than drinking out of the toilet," she said out loud. "Not that you seem to mind,

Dog."

She looked to her left where Dog should be, expecting an empty space. But someone was there. It was the mutant freak. He was small and hunched monkey-like, his skin so pale she could see through it to his veins. Half his face was shaped like a person, like she saw herself in the mirror. The other half was a monster with bulges in his cheeks and lips.

She froze.

The creature pulled back, his big, weird eyes staring without blinking.

She patted at her pockets. She couldn't remember what killing weapon she brought, or where she put it. Then she saw what he was holding in his hands. Her backpack.

"Where did you get that?" she said, angry that his mutant germs were getting all over it.

He just held out the backpack, and inched closer.

"No!" she said. "Bad dog!"

The creature stopped.

She moved away from him a step, watching him. He didn't follow. "Good boy," she said.

He perked up, darted toward her.

"No!" she said again.

The creature dropped her backpack, pulled himself into a ball and rolled to his side, hugging his arms around his knees. He wailed. The kind of noise she made the morning she found Daddy in the treehouse, when he wouldn't wake up.

She slapped her hands over her ears. That sound

made her sad, and she didn't want to be any sadder than she already was. "Please don't do that," she said. "Please."

The creature went quiet. He uncurled from his ball shape. He made a sound like a puppy.

She stared at him. She'd never seen one of them so close. Usually they were shapes and shadows in the distance. This one didn't seem all that scary, now that she got a look at him. But Daddy would not want her to get any closer.

The little freak just stared at her.

"Why don't you wear clothes?" she asked.

He just stared some more and picked his nose. Even Dog had better manners than that.

"I want my backpack," she said. She pointed at it. Then she pointed at the mutant. "You, move over there." She pointed again. "Over there."

The creature looked at the end of her finger. Then he scrabbled on his knobby legs, hands dragging along beside him, and sat onto the bottom of a grocery rack some feet away.

"I guess that's good enough," she said. She kept her eyes on him, suspicious, and inched toward her backpack. Once she touched the fabric, she grabbed it and ran.

She heard him squawk and heard his pattering feet behind her. She jumped over rotten food boxes, out through the broken glass door, and into the street.

She tried to run all the way back home. Her legs wouldn't do it. She got as far as the edge of the city, where the concrete was covered in mounds of grass. She didn't even know her legs stopped working until she saw the ground coming up at her. She landed hard and skidded, face-down.

When she finally came to a stop, she tried to push to her feet. She could only get to her knees. She looked at her hands. They were scuffed and bleeding. Her cheek felt scraped. She tasted blood where her teeth bit into her bottom lip.

Her stomach clenched. It was empty and hurting. Her bones inside her wanted water. Her head felt heavy and full of rocks.

She realized she was crying.

She heard shuffling and knew what it was without even looking. Maybe it really was her time, finally. She'd tried to make it happen yesterday but was too afraid. She wasn't afraid now. If the mutant freaks were going to eat her skin, she hoped they would at least wait until she was sleeping and couldn't feel it.

She looked to her left to tell that to the little mutant, but what she whispered was, "Why didn't he take me with him?"

The mutant tilted his head, the way Dog did sometimes. He made a sound from his throat with a quiet click in it.

"Why?" she said, louder. Her tears made her cheek sting. Her sadness made her heart sting.

The mutant growled. He was louder too.

"He should have taken me with him!" she cried.

The mutant made a loud sound like a bark.

Her sadness and anger and fear all mixed together

to make her yell at the sky, "Why didn't you take me with you?" Her body shook. Her chest squeezed. Her insides spasmed like she was going to throw up, but all that came out was rage. She didn't have words anymore, just feelings that turned into screaming.

The mutant tipped back his head and howled.

She squeezed her eyes closed and screamed and screamed. The mutant howled and howled.

Then she was too tired to scream anymore. She drooped. She tipped over and fell to the ground. She saw the mutant beside her. He had gone quiet too. He laid on his side.

They stayed there watching each other, their cheeks pressed to the ground. She didn't say anything. Neither did he.

Behind him, another shriveled little creature stepped out from a shadow. Then another. Down from crags in the city's broken places. Up from caved-in holes.

She pushed up to her knees again. There were more mutants than she had fingers to count. They were covered in lumps. They had patches of hair in strange places. None of them wore clothes. She could see there were girls and boys. They just stared at her and stood far away.

Then one with hands that were too big held up a can of food. He passed it to another, who passed it to another. A girl freak, all hunched over, carried the can to the creature near her; the little monkey mutant lying on the ground.

He hopped up and scooted toward her. He set the

can on the ground in front of her knees.

She recognized it, then. It was her can of pork and beans she'd left by Dog's big fire.

The can was a pop top. She grabbed it and pulled it open. Then she scooped her fingers in the sticky beans and shoveled them into her mouth. She ate and ate until the can was empty. She tipped it up and drained the last of the sauce.

She burped. She felt better.

The monkey mutant watched her eat. Now he backed up and turned toward the other mutants. They began moving as a group, back into the city. He paused and looked back. He moved a few feet and paused and looked again.

She was pretty sure she was supposed to follow. Daddy would have told her not to go, that they were leading her to the place where they would eat her. She stood up anyway and scuffled on her tired feet to follow.

Monkey mutant reached up for her hand. His skin was rubbery and cool, and she flinched. He made a sad noise. She stuck out her hand and let him take it.

He led her toward the group of mutants, and then they all shifted forward. They seemed to climb and jump and pick their way through the rubble as though they were part of it.

Monkey mutant kept her on a low path that, at first, just looked like every other ruined street. Then she realized there was a thin layer of rock dust settled into a sort of pattern around buildings. She'd gotten used to the feel of Monkey's fingers. She didn't mind his hand after all.

The other mutants disappeared from sight over a crest of slats and blocks. At the base of the crest, she saw broken furniture. Two chunks of seats, all connected together in a row, laid across each other in an X. She'd never been to this part of the city.

"Where are we going?" she asked.

Monkey pulled at her hand. She had to duck under a beam, and step over a puddle. Just as she realized what she'd stepped over, she saw the other mutants. They were splashing each other from a stream of water that leaked between concrete and rotting lumber wood. On the inside part of the ruined structure, a large pipe stuck out of the ground. It burbled up water like a fountain.

"Water!" she said, because she was so shocked.

Monkey led her to the pipe and let go of her hand. He slurped at the water, and then looked at her expectantly. She dropped to her knees and drank and drank until her belly sloshed.

That night, in her crumpled rail car, she laid on her mattress, on her side. Her insides were warm from food and the water from the pipe. She was drowsy, in a good way. Comfortable.

The little mutant had followed her home. He stared at her now, in the evening light pouring in through the open door. He made a clicking sound. She was becoming used to that. He crawled onto the mattress to lay against her legs.

"No," she said. She stood up and walked to the mound of blankets covered in dog fur. "You sleep here."

The mutant scrabbled over to the blankets and sniffed them. He laid onto them, resting his chin on a bumpy fold.

"Your name is Monkey," she said. "I hope that's okay."

Monkey's eyelids drooped closed.

"I'm going to have to think of names for all your friends," she said.

He nuzzled his face deeper into the blankets.

Girl patted his head. Then she walked back to her mattress and laid down again. She watched him, made sure he stayed put. He did.

"Good night, Monkey," she said. She smiled a little. "You're a good boy."

The Scowship Enterprise

Rusty Sims used to like pizza. He'd sit around with his friends, inhaling cigars and exhaling poker chips, calling it 'za and eating pepperoni because it was the Sunday night thing to do, each triangle slice pointing at him like arrows so the universe would know who to revolve around. He'd been full of power, then. Opportunities.

Now Rusty ate pizza because it was always on sale at MegaMart.

He wrestled with the cellophane around his freeze-dried breakfast and scowled at the green flecks leering at him through the wrapper. "You know I hate green peppers," he said to his wife, Muna, who was pouring her breakfast smoothie from the blender to a glass.

Muna wore yoga pants and a sports bra. She must

have already had her online workout with her personal trainer, because her shoulders glistened, and her hairline was damp. "You'll want a knife for that wrapper," said Muna. "You keep yanking at it like that and you'll—"

The cellophane split like a seam on Rusty's old jeans and catapulted dried mozzarella flakes all over the floor.

"Nice, Dad," said his son, Harper, as he shuffled past in the hallway.

Rusty threw the pizza into the steamer and ground his teeth.

"I'm going to Jake's," said Harper's voice as the front door opened.

"Again?" called Muna. "Did you sign onto class at all yesterday?"

"Yeah, from Jake's. Oh, and I got a weird netmail doc. I think was supposed to be yours, Mom. I forwarded it. See you later."

"What makes you think it's--?" Muna started to ask, but Jake shut the door. She shook her head and turned. "I've got to sign onto work." She nodded toward the mess on the floor. "WhiskVac's in the closet. Don't miss your shuttle." She carried her smoothie toward the spare room to log on to another workday at her virtual office.

Rusty envied her for that. She never had to use a public shuttle to get to work. Six days a week Rusty climbed into a tuna can; that's what he called them, not just because they were clanky metal transports, but because they always stunk like a day-old sandwich.

He was lifted up and over Atlantic Avenue by creaky hydraulics to stare down through the shuttle's glass floor at fishing piers he never visited and ocean waves he never swam in. Someday, he always said.

Rusty was a garbage scowship controller, one of the least glamorous jobs in America, and one he had to leave the house to perform.

Perform. A good word for it, because he felt like a trained monkey most days.

He followed Muna into the room where she worked. He peered in, just as she closed the netmail window on her computer screen. He thought he'd caught sight of a pink background with twirling flowers, and he was about to ask, when the steamer buzzed that his breakfast was ready.

He darted to the kitchen, picked the green bits off his soggy pizza, hollered a good-bye to Muna, and shoved in a mouthful on his way out.

He was a half block from the shuttle drop when the sky released a growl. "Don't you dare," he said to the bloated clouds. The sky just growled again, and then vomited gallons.

Rusty slopped through the gates at Cape Canaveral into the lobby of Unified Waste Management Enterprises. His shoes squeaked, his pants chafed, and his shirt was glued to his middle-aged paunch.

He waved distractedly to a security guard he didn't

recognize, and then to Lamphrey Peterson, the admin assistant, who was refilling his water bottle at a drinking fountain. Rusty wasn't paying attention to whether anyone waved back.

He turned left into the controller room. "You smell like a wet, day-old sandwich," said his shift mate Bob Landen, his voice echoing in the huge chamber.

"Thanks. You too."

It was just him and Bob this morning, surrounded by panels and lights and walls covered in eight-foot screens; billions of dollars of decaying spacewalking equipment from when the United States used to blast astronauts into the cosmos. Now, Bob and Rusty used the equipment to blast Earth's garbage into orbit.

"Got a loader stuck on the platform this morning, can't unhinge the gripper," said Bob.

"Nice of third shift to leave it for us." Rusty punched a button on the coffee machine.

"One of us will have to climb up and manually release it, I guess."

Rusty hit the button again. "Should we draw straws?"

Bob waggled the treadle on the control panel, then clucked his tongue. "No use, it won't give." Then he stood. "If you're trying for coffee, don't bother. I couldn't get that to give, either."

Rusty slammed his fist at the button. "Unbelievable!"

"Yeah, they can send a man to the moon, but they can't make a reliable coffee pot," said Bob, grinning at the inside joke.

Although it wasn't very "inside". Everyone knew how the space program had flopped, how minor advancements came nowhere near rationalizing the astronomical costs. In the end, private business bought out another defunct government program. No one was trying to get to the moon anymore.

"So, I'm thinking," said Bob. "You're already drenched, what's the point in me climbing all the way up there in this weather? You go unhinge the gripper, and I'll go get us some real joe."

Rusty pressed at his eyes with his fingertips.

"I'll get that mocha blend you like."

"Fine," said Rusty. His mood couldn't get much worse, anyway. "But you're paying, and it better be one of those jumbo sizes."

"Sure, no problem, buddy." Bob slapped him in the arm, and then reached for his overcoat near the door. "I won't be long. Be careful out there."

The Florida rain hit Rusty's face like it was being shot from a cannon. He squinted to see, lunging his way toward the platform while the wind tried to knock him off his feet.

When he got to the loader, the problem was so obvious it was stupid. The enormous loader truck had been driven too close to the scow's fill rim, and its swiveling collection arm was trapped between the scow and the front of the truck. The arm was wheezing and grinding, trying to pull free, but it only slammed the truck back and forth, wedging itself tighter.

Whoever abandoned their lousy parking job had left the keys in the ignition. Rusty climbed the loader steps to haul himself behind the wheel. He wiped rainwater from his eyes, then turned the key. The engine snarled, and warm air blasted from the dashboard vents, fluttering his soaked shirt collar.

The moment he released the clutch, the rig lurched and the robotic arm heaved loose. It flailed backward then ricocheted forward, its gripper clamps wildly chewing the air, and smashed down hard onto the windshield. Glass shattered; razorblade sharp. The clamps lunged toward Rusty's face, but he ducked, and he felt them around his arm instead.

He heard, and felt, his shoulder snap. Then he was yanked through the windshield.

Muna Sims sat in her office chair, watching her animated netmail card forwarded by Harper. Dancing pink flowers read "your mine" across her computer screen. Misspelled. She rolled her eyes.

Then her phone buzzed with a text alert. She tapped the inbox link to open a photo; it was a picture from the inside of a public transport shuttle. On the seat was a cardboard carrier holding two tall paper cups bearing a "Carpe Café" coffee shop logo.

Muna felt a jolt of anticipation. Too late to change her mind now. Not that it was an option, anyway.

Then she got a closer look at her text, and saw she wasn't the only number that had received the photo. The other person was LP@UWME. "Bob," Muna muttered quietly. "You are a fucking idiot."

Lamphrey Peterson was walking a memo to the head office when he felt a buzz in his pocket. He tapped the flesh-colored nub in his ear to connect a call. "Unified Waste Management Enterprises," he said. When there was nothing but dead air, he realized the buzz had come from his personal phone, not the office lines. He disconnected his office receiver, slipped a yellow sheet into the slot on his boss's door, and then dug out his phone from his slacks. He opened a text with an attached photo that showed a couple of coffees from a local café in a paper carrier.

Lamphrey looked around himself in the empty hallway, in case someone was out of sight, snickering at some joke they forgot to explain to him. Then he expanded the photo larger and peered closer.

A couple of blurry fingers blocked the upper left corner of the photo, but Lamphrey recognized the fake ruby on a class ring on the pinkie. Bob Landen had a ring like that, and he wore it on his pinkie.

Lamphrey stood there, puzzling over the mysterious text. It wasn't really Bob's style to flirt, and he certainly didn't know Lamphrey's favorite: iced cappuccino. Or did he? Lamphrey finally walked toward the control room to see if Bob was there.

When Lamphrey swung open the door to the control room, he sucked in a breath. An eight-foot screen showed Rusty Sims, splayed across the hood of a loading rig on a scowship platform. The rig's robotic arm had gone haywire, beating at glass and metal, showering Rusty's limp body in shrapnel. Lamphrey tapped the panic button on his ear nub and threw himself at the control panel, frantically texting in an emergency request.

"Emergency received," said a voice in his ear. "Verify Peterson, Unified Waste Management Enterprises control room, North Atlantic Avenue, Cape Canaveral," said the voice.

"Verified!" Lamphrey shouted back.

Lamphrey ran to the regulator panel and hit buttons to disconnect the signal to the loader arm. No response. He typed in commands to force a power shut down. Still nothing. He reached for the control treadle on Bob's workstation to wrench it loose; he knew if he could break the treadle, it might trigger a network failure. It wasn't supposed to work that way, but at the moment, he hoped to god it would.

There was a coin jammed into the receiver slot, forcing the treadle "on." Lamphrey yanked and tugged, but the thing wouldn't budge. He punched it with his fist. He kicked it. Finally, he hoisted an office chair and slammed it. The treadle broke off. The panel lights went dim, first on Bob's workstation, then on Rusty's, beside it, and then, on the screen, he saw the load arm drop motionless against the hood of the rig.

Bob appeared in the doorway, holding a cardboard carrier and two tall cups of coffee. "What the-?"

"It's Rusty," said Lamphrey. "The loading rig malfunctioned."

"The rig?" asked Bob, gaping.

Lamphrey and Bob watched the screen. Platform crewmembers gathered around the rig. One of them climbed up but was shooed away by emergency workers. Then the screen blinked off, too. Cooling fans in the panels whirred to quiet. Ceiling lights went dark, and red-tinged emergency lighting took over.

Lamphrey, breathless and trembling, looked at Bob.

"I was getting coffee," said Bob, holding up the cups. "Our coffee maker is busted."

Lamphrey could already hear the confused bustle in the hallway from executives being forced from their cushy offices to ask what the hell was going on. He dreaded facing them, and the OSHA paperwork that was going to be a bitch and a half to deal with. It had been an open secret for a long time about the control panel's safety flaws, but Lamphrey had just busted that secret wide open. He'd probably just made career-ending choice.

On the upside, if he got fired, he wouldn't have to deal with the OSHA paperwork.

Bob was still standing and holding the coffees.

Lamphrey wearily reached up to take one out

of the carrier. He walked toward the head office and sipped. He frowned. Definitely not iced cappuccino.

That's when it hit him. There was a *coin* jammed in the treadle slot. And he was sure this morning he'd seen the coffee machine in the control room unplugged, with the cord lying on the floor.

Rusty's mouth felt like flannel. His shoulder throbbed--no, his whole body throbbed. He felt a thin mattress beneath him, hot sunlight breathing on his face. When he opened his eyes, it was like trying to see through grape gelatin. "Where am I?"

"Hi, honey," said Muna. She loomed closer, her shape a blob. "You're in the hospital. You've had a terrible accident, but you're going to be okay."

He was surprised at the relief he felt at the sound of her voice.

"Do you need me to close the window shade?" she asked. She was already twisting the shade rod before Rusty had a chance to reply.

As the sunlight was pinched off, his hospital room came into focus around him. Gray walls, gray bed frame, gray tubes stabbed into his arms. Private room. Who was footing the bill for that?

Muna gently moved aside wires and hoses affixed to his chest. Then the bed shifted, and he smelled lilac soap as she settled beside him. He couldn't remember the last time she pressed against him like that.

"They had to insert a rod into your arm," she said. "Plus, you have a broken rib. The doctors say it's a miracle you don't have a concussion."

"An accident," Rusty said. "The scowship."

"Yes. A malfunction with the loading rig. Lamphrey stopped it. One more minute and... well, I'm trying not to think about that." She released a soft breath and rested her head onto his shoulder.

Rusty tried to piece together what he could. He had been drenched from rain in the control room. Bob said something about coffee. "You said Lamphrey stopped it?" he asked.

"It was his fast thinking that shut down the power," said Muna. She stroked her fingers along his chin. He couldn't remember the last time she'd done that, either. "Let's not tell anyone you're awake yet," she said. "I like that we're here alone together."

He tried to smile, but it hurt. When she shifted against him again, he could feel her staring. He became aware of bandages on his face. "What is it?"

"I'm just imagining you with rugged scars," she said. Her gaze was heavy, intense. "I didn't think I was going to see you after today."

"When I saw that load arm come through the windshield, *I* didn't think I was going to see anybody after today," said Rusty.

"You and I need to agree on what we're going to say."

"What?" said Rusty.

"Our lawyer advised us to say nothing at all about

what happened, how it happened, or whatever part you played," she said. "Not yet."

"Our what?" Rusty tried to turn his head to get a better look at her face, but it stabbed pain into his neck. "When did we get a lawyer?"

"Yesterday," said Muna. She laid her hand on his bandaged chest. "Unified Waste reps showed up here in the waiting room. I could tell they were positioning, so I thought I should be prepared."

"Prepared for what?" Rusty asked.

Muna pushed up to her elbow to look down at him. "You had an accident at work, honey. You almost died."

That's when the reality began settling down onto him, pressing him against the bed. Or maybe it was the pain meds wearing off. Until that moment, he'd been thinking of this as a temporary setback, like a twisted ankle. A couple weeks off work, then back to the grind.

"Work injury," Rusty said, practicing the sound of it. He knew guys who had retired on workman's comp payouts.

"Yeah," said Muna. "And our lawyer thinks there's an excellent case for negligence, too."

Rusty remembered the truck, then. The stupid parking job. Definitely negligence. "When do I meet this lawyer? Does he think there's money in this? Like, *money* money?"

"That's what he says," said Muna. "As long as we let him do all the talking. But…" Her face went thoughtful. "The police have been prowling around here, too," she said.

"Wait. Wait a minute," said Rusty. "The police?"

Muna rolled away from him and slid sideways to stand up off the bed. "They're investigating," said Muna. "It's nonsense. They just want to feel important."

"Why would they to talk to me?" said Rusty. "I barely remember anything."

"Perfect," said Muna, and she smiled. "We'll stick with that." She smoothed her blouse, a gray one that buttoned up her neck, and her black skirt. With her hair pulled into a bun at the base of her head, she looked prim and subdued, not all her usual style. "I need to pick up Harper from the Johnsons', but I'll be back later to-"

The door swung open. Rusty got a blast of noise from the hospital hallway; beeping machines, the clack of keyboards, hushed voices. A slender redheaded nurse in scrubs walked in, a stethoscope around his neck, and stopped short in surprise. "Oh, Mr. Sims, you're awake."

A tall black woman in khakis and a blazer appeared in the doorway. "What's that? He's awake?"

"Yes, Detective, but that doesn't mean he's well enough to answer questions," said the nurse, moving to block her.

Muna laid her hand on Rusty's forearm.

"It will only take a minute," said the detective. She pushed into the room, shouldering the nurse out of the way. "Morning, Mrs. Sims," she said, nodding at Muna.

"Detective," said Muna, her voice flat.

"Rusty Sims?" asked the detective, coming to stand beside the bed.

"Unless Mrs. Sims is in here with some other guy who had his ass beat by a scowship loader," Rusty answered.

The woman pulled a smooth, brown disc from her pocket and clipped it to her lapel. "I'm Detective Cynthia Montgomery from the Brevard County Police," she said. "This is a recording device for official record. I'd like to ask you some questions related to the incident at Unified Waste Management Enterprises on Tuesday, September first."

Muna gave a pleading look to the nurse. "Detective, I don't think it's a good time-"

"Mr. Sims looks wide awake to me," said the detective.

The nurse rolled a machine to the foot of the bed. He extracted a cord from it and plugged it into a port on the bed frame. "I need to check Mr. Sims's vitals. He shouldn't be talking or moving around."

"Can't it wait?" asked Detective Montgomery.

"Are you asking the hospital to withhold care?" said Muna. She leaned in to speak directly into the brown disc on the detective's blazer. "On record?"

The detective frowned. She removed the disc and dropped it into her blazer's inside pocket. "The longer you put this off, the more suspicious it looks."

"A suspicious *accident*?" asked Rusty.

The detective was looking directly at Muna. The woman's steely expression made Rusty look at Muna, too.

"Our family has been through an upheaval," said

Muna. "My husband has just awoken from a *coma*. I've been caring single-handedly for our son, while wondering how I was going to tell him he lost his dad."

"But he didn't lose him," said Detective Montgomery.

"Thanks to modern medicine," said Muna, and looked at the nurse with a heartwarming smile. The nurse blushed and turned his attention to tapping things into the machine plugged into Rusty's bed. Muna looked back at the detective; her smile vanished, replaced by pursed lips and a steady lock on the detective's eyes. "But no thanks to you, Detective, so I don't know why you think we owe you one minute of our time."

There was a long silence. Rusty could hear the bustle of the hallway again, heard a chirping whistle on the window ledge. The nurse steadily tapped commands into the machine, with no outward awareness of the discomfort in the room, except for a twitch under his left eye.

Rusty didn't realize how accustomed he'd become to Muna's control issues until now; seeing them directed at someone else.

It was also in the silence that Rusty realized he was suspicious of Muna, too. Not just because of her uncharacteristic cuddling in the hospital bed, not because of her widow-in-mourning outfit, or even because she'd been apparently practicing telling their son he was dead. What really got him was that she'd called them a *family*. He didn't think he'd ever heard her say that before.

Eventually, the detective took a step back. The sign of defeat. Rusty wanted to comfort the cop, tell her it was all right. That it's just how Muna was when she'd already made up her mind.

"You seem to be feeling just fine, Mrs. Sims," said the detective. "I can't see why you wouldn't be able to have a chat with me at the station."

"I'll need to talk with my lawyer about that," Muna said.

"Right." The detective looked at Rusty, gave him a nod. "We'll speak again, Mr. Sims. Good day."

"What a brute," said Muna at the detective's back, way before she was out of earshot. "It's like they train women to be twice the bully as the men." Then she walked toward the door, too. "I'm sorry you had to witness that, Kevin," she said to the nurse. Then she smiled at Rusty. "I hope she hasn't upset you, honey. You need to rest. I'll be back later. Love you." She closed the door.

"Have I really been in a coma?" Rusty asked Kevin.

Kevin hesitated. "Anesthesia is a sort of drug-induced coma," he said. "So, you could call it that, sure."

"What else could you call it?" asked Rusty.

"Sleeping," said Nurse Kevin. He pushed a gray button on the wheeled machine. "Now let's get those vitals again. I'm not happy about your blood pressure reading."

◇

Detective Cynthia Montgomery flashed her badge at the coffee shop waitress and then sat on a stool near a glass case filled with plastic-wrapped brownies. Moments later the girl came from behind the counter. She wore jeans and a t-shirt reading "Carpe Café" and a small, pink apron around her waist. Early twenties, maybe. The girl wore a messy bun, and a strand of her brunette hair had come loose. She tucked it behind her ear. A nervous gesture. "You asked for me, officer?"

"Are you Katie Sparks?" When the girl nodded, Cynthia showed her a photo of Bob Landen on her phone. "Did this man come in here two days ago, on September first?"

Katie leaned in to get a look at the photo. Her strand drooped in front of her ear. She tucked it behind, again. "Um. Maybe? He looks like most people who come in here."

"He's not a regular, as far as you know?"

Katie shook her head. "No, sir. Ma'am," she quickly corrected.

Not the first time a witness had slipped on her gender. She joked at the station that she wasn't sure if it was the badge that confused people, or her cheap haircut. "He's an employee at United Waste," said Cynthia. "At Cape Canaveral, down the street."

"Oh." Katie smiled. "The scowship enterprise."

"The what?" Cynthia asked.

Katie's smile faded. "Sorry. That's what we call it around here." She moved her hand to tuck her strand behind her ear, but there was no loose hair to tuck. "But, um, yeah, we get a lot of people from there. A lot of orders for a catered basket for meetings and stuff."

"But not this guy?" Cynthia held up the photo again. Katie shook her head. "I don't remember him."

"Ok," said Cynthia. "Thanks."

Katie gave a half-smile, lingering awkwardly. She smoothed her hands down her apron.

"Are your brownies any good?" Cynthia asked, to break the silence.

"They're good, but our chocolate chip muffins are better," she said. "Let me get you one, on the house."

"Oh, thanks," said Cynthia.

While she waited, she surveyed the clientele. People with netbooks and netpads, typing or reading. The usual. The door opened and closed regularly, with a chime of bell. She wondered if the staff got so used to it, they didn't hear it anymore.

"Hi, Katie," said a customer at the counter. "Are your muffins fresh?"

Cynthia heard Katie's voice. "They sure are. Haven't seen you in a couple days."

"Yeah. Weird days at work."

"I hear you," said Katie.

"Can you put those in a box today?" asked the customer. "They're for a friend."

Cynthia watched the customer tap his fingers on the counter while he waited. Patient, but tense. Nice eyes, expensive haircut. Not from a barbershop, like where Cynthia went.

A ribbon-tied box passed into the customer's

hands, and he smiled. Nice smile, too. She watched him walk toward the door.

Katie came her to her seat then, with a muffin on a glass plate. "Lamphrey works at United Waste. *He's* one of our regulars."

"Lamphrey?" Cynthia said. She stood. "Hey, thanks, Katie." She grabbed the muffin off the plate and hurried through the crowded space.

Outside, she spotted her target walking to the Atlantic South Street stop. She tailed him. She mindlessly took a bite of muffin, then paused, and looked at it. It *was* damn good. She shoved the rest into her mouth, and after her target climbed into a shuttle, she hopped on the next one. She poked commands into the shuttle panel to track him, and as her pod rose up and behind him, following, she pretended to be interested in the view.

Rusty had lost track of time. Pain meds kept him drowsy, but he couldn't remember sleeping. The sun seemed to be in different places in the sky at different times through the blinds, but it didn't mean anything to him. He felt trapped in a time capsule while the world went on without him.

That's what would have happened, if he'd actually died. Everyone else would wake up, work, sleep, eat, and screw, the way they always had, while Rusty laid in a grave instead a hospital bed. Muna hadn't been back, like she said she would. Harper hadn't visited.

Maybe Rusty did die, and his afterlife was this endless cycle of being reminded that no one noticed he was gone.

There was a knock at the door, so soft Rusty wasn't sure if he'd imagined it. "Hello?" he called.

The door pushed open, and the face of Lamphrey Peterson peered around it. "Did I wake you up?" he asked.

Rusty had an unexpected rush of emotion; gratitude, for Lamphrey's quick thinking at work, and now, for being here at this moment. "Hey there, Lamphrey," he called. "I was awake."

Lamphrey closed the door behind himself and walked gingerly toward the bed. "I'm not very comfortable in hospitals," he said.

"That makes two of us," said Rusty.

Lamphrey's eyes took in the sight of Rusty's bandages around his chest and arms. Kevin had removed Rusty's face gauze earlier, but he hadn't seen himself in a mirror. He was suddenly self-conscious. Lamphrey didn't seem put off, only sad. "You look like you hurt," he said.

"Yeah, but they're pumping me with top shelf meds," said Rusty. "The good shit."

"Oh," said Lamphrey. He chuckled. "Maybe you could hook me up, then."

"I'll see what I can do. I know a guy." Rusty chuckled, too, but it choked off when it squeezed pain against his rib. "His name is Kevin," he said, and made a mental note to never exhale like that again. Ever.

The door swung open again, and Kevin backed into the room, pulling a rolling cart.

"There he is now," said Rusty.

"There who is now?" asked Kevin. He circled to move the cart in front of himself but stopped when he spotted Lamphrey. "Oh. Well, hi."

"Kevin, this is Lamphrey Peterson," said Rusty.

"*The* Lamphrey? From work?" asked Kevin. He smiled and put his hand beside his mouth in a pretend whisper. "You didn't mention he's handsome."

"You know me?" asked Lamphrey.

"Everyone at the nurse's station knows you," said Kevin. "You're a hero."

"Well... I just..." Lamphrey stammered. "I'm not..."

"A hero with gifts," said Kevin, eyeing the box in Lamphrey's hands. Rusty hadn't even noticed it until that moment. It was pink and tied with ribbon.

Lamphrey seemed to suddenly remember the box, too. He held it toward Rusty. "Best chocolate chip muffins this side of the Atlantic," he said.

"For me?" asked Rusty.

His expression must have betrayed his surprise, because Lamphrey shrank back. "I didn't think to ask if you even like muffins."

"If they're the kind you sneak us as leftovers from board meetings, I do," said Rusty. He held out his bandaged hand toward the box. "Thank you," he said.

Lamphrey smiled. Rusty watched him grab a table

on wheels, set the muffin box onto it, and push it up against Rusty's bed. It was a small movement in a flash of a moment, but it was suddenly familiar. He'd watched Lamphrey at work, week after week, year after year, arranging, organizing, meticulously setting up tables for meetings, taking them back down. Lamphrey kept a vase in the control room and would bring begonias from his yard to keep it filled. He created gift bags for head office visitors, families, CEOs. United wouldn't even have holiday parties, if not for Lamphrey seeing to it. Decorating. Arranging caterers. Making sure people were cared for.

Making sure Rusty was cared for. He became uncomfortably aware that Lamphrey had been more of a part of his life than he'd ever noticed.

"Lam," said Rusty, his hand still outstretched, bandaged palm open.

Lamphrey saw Rusty's hand. Confusion passed over his face, but he rested his fingers on Rusty's palm.

"*Thank you*," said Rusty.

Lamphrey smiled, soft and warm. He tipped his head. His eyes traveled over Rusty's features. "I'm glad I was there."

Rusty was startled to realize it, but he was glad he was alive, too.

A noise, a short clank of metal, sounded near the foot of Rusty's bed.

Lamphrey looked at Kevin as though he'd forgotten the nurse was there.

Kevin was holding the metal dongle at the end of

a blue cord. He was regarding them both with upraised brows and a soft smile.

"Oh," said Lamphrey to Kevin. "There are enough muffins to share."

Kevin held up a hand. "No, no, three's a crowd," he said. Then he wheeled his cart right back out the door, with a lingering smile over his shoulder.

Rusty watched the door close. He rested back against the inclined mattress. "I think he likes you," he said to Lamphrey.

"The nurse?" Lamphrey shook his head. He reached for the box and cleared his throat. "Let's get you a muffin."

Another knock on the door. A fist, this time, pounding swift and sudden. Lamphrey startled and put a hand to his chest.

Rusty's room was beginning to feel less like a grave and more like Brevard Transit at rush hour. At least it was preferable.

"Mr. Sims?" Detective Montgomery didn't wait for an invitation. She strode into the room. Rusty watched her eyes as they roved over Lamphrey, the pink muffin box, and Rusty's bandages. She pulled a chair from the corner and sat, and then retrieved her smooth, brown disk from her pocket to pin it to her shirt collar.

Lamphrey watched the woman and turned a quizzical face to Rusty.

"This is Detective Montgomery," Rusty explained.

"Oh! Good," said Lamphrey. He pulled the ribbon off the box of muffins, opened it, and offered it toward her.

The detective paused her motion. Rusty guessed she didn't often hear someone sound happy to see her. She looked down at the muffins. "Had one at the café. Those are damn good," she said.

"Right?" Lamphrey beamed a smile. He returned the box to the table.

Rusty got a good whiff of them, and his mouth watered. He reached for one, took a large bite.

"Something's going on, isn't it?" asked Lamphrey. "I mean, I'm not sure how or why, but... it's hard to actually say it. I think someone hurt Rusty on purpose."

"You're Lamphrey," said the detective, clearly unaccustomed, also, to having someone initiate an interview with *her*. "Lamphrey Peterson? You work with Mr. Sims at United Waste?"

"Yes," said Lamphrey. "Well, I did."

Rusty stopped chewing his muffin.

"Did?" asked the detective, before Rusty could say the same thing.

"Lamphrey is just a nickname that stuck. My legal name is Lamani," he said.

The detective tapped the disk on her collar. "Noted," she said. "What do you mean, 'did'?"

Lamphrey glanced at Rusty. "It's not official yet. I mean, the publicity is hitting the fan, so the head office is tiptoeing, but they've netmailed me a long, poetic resignation letter I'm supposed to sign."

Rusty nearly spit out his last mouthful of muffin. "They fired you for saving my life?"

"It's more about *how* I saved you," said Lamphrey. "But it's okay. I don't have any regrets."

Lamphrey's eyes met Rusty's, and Rusty felt it again; gratitude. It was kind of nice, now that he was beginning to recognize it. "Still," Rusty said, quietly, while Lamphrey studied his face. "Don't sign anything. Not yet."

"Okay," said Lamphrey.

Detective Montgomery sat forward in her chair and rested her elbows on her knees. "What makes you think someone hurt Rusty on purpose, Mr. Peterson?"

"The coffee machine in the control room worked just fine," said Lamphrey. "Later in the day I plugged it in and tried it."

"It was unplugged?" asked the detective. "You're one hundred percent sure?"

"Hand on the bible in a court of law," said Lamphrey.

"Jesus," said Rusty. "You think it was Bob?" He had worked beside the guy for nearly seven years. They weren't friends, exactly, but they got along well, or so he thought.

"He might have assumed it was broken without noticing the cord," the detective said. "And no one witnessed who sabotaged the control panel, so it's all circumstantial for now." She laced her fingers together, still leaning forward. "What I am sure about is your life insurance policy."

"Life insurance?" The bandages around his chest grew too tight. He heard his pulse in his ears.

"Mr. Sims, eight months ago, you and your wife tripled the value of your life insurance by raising the payout for the accidental death or dismemberment clause."

The detective's gaze burned into Rusty's face. He went hot, then cold. "I didn't sign any life insurance paperwork," he said.

The detective stood and withdrew a folded piece of paper from her pocket. She opened it and offered it to them. "This is the signature page of the contract. Your wife signed on the left, you signed on the right."

Lamphrey took the paper and frowned at it. "I can tell you, Detective Montgomery, that is not Rusty's handwriting." He held it up for Rusty to see.

Rusty eyed the signatures. He knew Muna's. The second one was close to his own, but not close enough. His head spun. She'd really done it. He often said it out loud, to Muna. To other people in front of Muna. He'd said, one of these days she'll get sick of me, and I'll disappear. He'd said it sarcastically, but a part of him had always known she never loved him. Not as much as she was in love with herself, anyway. He knew if she wanted something badly enough, she'd hurt anyone to get it. Still. He wanted to be wrong.

"You can prove it's a forgery, I assume," said the detective, taking back the paper, and folding it again.

"I can, easily," said Lamphrey. "Rusty's signature is all over forms and paperwork at United Waste. There's his tax exemption forms, his payroll registration, every delivery log from every shift he's worked…"

The detective nodded. "I'll need copies."

"No problem," said Lamphrey.

Rusty became aware that he'd been silent for a long time. "Sorry," he said, looking up to Detective Montgomery's face. "It's a lot to take in."

"Of course, it is," said Lamphrey.

"Do you know how long you'll be hospitalized, Mr. Sims?" asked the detective.

The abrupt shift took Rusty a moment to catch up. "A few days. No specifics yet. Why?"

She unpinned the small disk from her collar and returned it to her pocket. "All I have is a hunch, and, as I said, circumstance. My gut says Bob Landen had opportunity, and your wife had motive, but other than attempted calls and unanswered texts from Bob's phone to hers, there's nothing to put them together."

"What does that mean?" asked Rusty.

"Can I help in some way? I could talk to Bob, maybe," said Lamphrey.

The detective shook her head. "I'd rather not tip him off. Not yet. But come into the station in the morning. The precinct on Weatherly, by the fire station," she said. "Bring what you've got with Rusty's signature."

"Sure," said Lamphrey.

"I might have an idea. I'll have to clear it with the chief," she said. "Thank you for your time." She backed up a step and turned on her heel like a soldier.

She nearly bumped into Kevin, who was on his way in.

"Evening, Detective," said Kevin. He paused to

let her walk around his rolling cart, and then pushed it on wobbly wheels to the foot of Rusty's bed and smiled at him. "You're Mister Popular today." Kevin removed an empty plastic bag hanging from a hook off the footboard and swapped in a full bag from his cart. "What's your pain level, Mr. Sims?" he asked.

"Be more specific," said Rusty. "You mean physical or emotional?"

"Lucky for you, Tramadol will help with both," said Kevin.

"I should let you rest," said Lamphrey. He patted Rusty's arm, then quietly retreated toward the door.

He hadn't realized how much the previous dose had worn off until the Tramadol was freewheeling through his veins again. It gave his brain a chance to work around the pain from his chest and shoulder, making his thoughts bright and sharp. "Actually, Lam," he said. "Can you stay?"

Lamphrey paused. "Are you sure?"

"If you're able," said Rusty. "Yes. I'm sure." The truth--about how his death was more valuable to Muna than his life--was hanging in the room like a thundercloud, and he didn't want to be alone with it.

"I can stay," said Lamphrey. He pulled over the chair the detective had used and sat down by Rusty's side.

"Thank you," said Rusty. At least that's what he tried to say. His moment of clarity was brief; he was beginning to float.

"He'll be a little out of it," he heard Kevin say, and

heard the rolling cart and the sound of the door.

"You still with me?" Lamphrey asked.

Rusty fought against the drowse trying to take him. He forced his eyes open, found Lamphrey's face. "I'm here."

Lamphrey looked down. "This is hard to say."

"I'm so high right now, it's a good time to tell me," said Rusty.

"Before, when you said thank you, and let me hold your hand…"

"I meant it," said Rusty.

Lamphrey stared for a long time. "Ok," he said. "What the hell. Here goes." He inched to edge of his chair toward Rusty. "When I saw you on that screen, I was scared for more than one reason. I was worried you were going to die before I had a chance to tell you how I feel about you."

Rusty's mind was too sluggish to process anything except this moment, right now, looking at Lamphrey. It was enough. "Not just you," he slurred.

"Wait, what?" Lamphrey stood up and leaned close to Rusty's face, searching his eyes. "Exactly how high are you?"

Rusty chuckled, his eyes unfocusing. His lids drooped shut.

"I want to kiss you," said Lamphrey. Lamphrey's face was near, but his voice went far away, mixed into a dream.

"Mmh," was all Rusty could manage.

He felt Lamphrey's lips brush the corner of his

mouth.

So that's what it was like; a kiss as a connection. As a reminder that Rusty did know what love was supposed to feel like. He tried again to open his eyes, but all he could do was smile. "Lam?"

"Mm?" Lamphrey said.

Rusty tried to say something clever and profound. He fell asleep before he had the chance.

"A coin?!" Muna punched Bob in the arm, where he sat beside her in the Brevard Public Transit shuttle. "You used a *coin* to jam the controls? Are you a complete fucking *idiot*?"

The shuttle swerved down on its hydraulic sticks toward Muna's address. Muna had been careful to never call Bob's phone number or meet him in a private vehicle. She had never even crossed the threshold of his home; no trace evidence or DNA to even suggest her part in a relationship with him. Just in case. Just in case something exactly like this happened.

"There was no way to get the control panel to stop communicating with the load arm. The thing was built to launch spaceships, Moon," said Bob.

She hated when he used her nickname. "Well, it doesn't exactly look like an accident now, does it?"

Bob just leaned back against his seat. His shoulders arched forward.

"A detective was there when Rusty woke up

Wednesday. That bitch is not going to make this easy." Muna watched Bob scratch at his balding temple. Had his hair always been so thin? Even Rusty still had hair she could run her fingers through. "Have they talked to you yet?" she asked. "Or to any other crew?"

"Calls have come into the head offices, but no one's told me what they're about," said Bob. "I know there's a lot of hush-hush because of the OSHA violations."

"The what?" Muna stood up and pressed the "hold" lever on the shuttle. The hydraulics froze, letting the shuttle compartment dangle above a cove in Satellite Beach.

"OSHA. Occupational Safety and--"

"I know what OSHA is, Bob," snapped Muna. "I want to hear about these violations."

Bob winced. He looked down through the glass floor. He shifted in his seat.

"Are you seriously afraid of getting in trouble with OSHA?" Muna crossed her arms. "More afraid than the trouble you're in, right now?"

Bob looked up at her with eyes the color of ashes. She'd always seen them as blue, but in this light, through the bars of the shuttle, they were pale. "I'm not afraid of OSHA. Head Office is. Lamphrey Peterson came in today to warn me they were pushing him out because of what he did. Look." He removed a small plastic case from his pocket and held it out.

"What?" Muna shrugged at it.

"The records they've requested he pull on me. They're gunning for me, too."

"Are you serious?" Muna stared at him, tried to understand how so much stupid could be crammed into such a small brain. "Head Office can't send you to prison, Bob."

Bob frowned. He dropped the plastic case into his shirt pocket, pouting.

"Okay," said Muna. She knew not to push him too far. He was too goddammed sensitive, but she still needed him for now. "So, what did Lamphrey do?" asked Muna.

"He shouldn't have been able to break the treadle. He knew it would, because that's one of the issues in the write-ups," he said. "The controls and the way they communicate with the launching pads is outdated. It's been cheaper for United to just pay the violations than to rebuild the system."

"Really." Muna sat beside him again and put her hand on his knee. "How long has this been going on?"

Bob shrugged. "For as long as I've been there. Ten years. Maybe longer." He looked at her hand, then into her face.

"Whose decision has it been to stall the upgrades?" asked Muna. She drew her hand up to his thigh, stroking.

Bob shrugged again. "Above my pay grade, Moon. I only hear things. I'm not in the room." He glanced down at her hand. "You thinking about a plan? You always get turned on when you're planning things."

"Do I?" she asked. She laughed quietly. She stood up and flipped the lever to get the shuttle moving again.

"Do I get to be a part of whatever it is?" asked Bob.

"Yes," she said. She held the shuttle's leather handle, standing by the door panel, watching the Levin Street stop come into view. The shuttle lowered into place, and the hydraulics pushed the transit pod into locking clamps. "Ok, give me about one minute after I leave, and then exit and walk down the street after me."

Bob stood up, just as the clamps took hold. He rocked on his feet. "You mean in the same direction?"

"Yep," she said. The shuttle door slid up and open, and she stepped down onto the sidewalk. She began walking the six blocks home, casually weaving through the pedestrian traffic going in and out of shops.

Moments later, she heard Bob's shuffling gait. She rolled her eyes. It had not been a minute. But never mind. She whirled on him, and gasped. "Bob?! Bob Landen?"

Bob stopped suddenly. His eyes widened. A few passersby looked between them with their brows arched. Curious, not concerned.

"What are you doing?" Muna said, louder. "Are you *following* me now?"

Bob took a step backward and bumped into a woman with groceries.

"Hey!" the woman said. "Watch it!"

More people looked in their direction. Bob saw them and looked back at Muna with fear in his eyes. "What...? What are you...?" he stammered.

"Get away from me!" Muna grabbed the arm of a young man who had stopped and was watching. "Do you have a phone? Can you call the police?"

The young man scrambled to dig into his pockets. "Yeah," he said. He pulled out a small metal frame and pressed it between his palms to make the call.

"Moon," said Bob. His voice was soft. Hurt.

"Why can't you just leave me alone?" cried Muna. An older woman with a floppy hat came to stand beside her. "Is he bothering you, sweetie?"

"He's been bothering me for weeks," said Muna, breaking into tears. The crowd of watchers was growing. "Calling me, sending me netmail docs. He's been threatening my husband." Then Muna gasped. "It was you! You hurt Rusty, didn't you?!"

"Now, wait a minute," said Bob. He took several more steps backward. Then he turned to run. He bumped into this person, that person, drawing scowls. He veered and disappeared around a corner.

"There, there," said the older woman, patting Muna's hand. She offered Muna a dainty handkerchief. "He's gone now. You're safe."

"Thank you," said Muna to the woman, to the young man. She heard the whirr-blip of an approaching scooter cop. "I'm sorry for making a scene. I was just so startled."

Individuals began milling back into motion, getting on with where they were going. A handful lingered, watching the cop approach on his rolling scooter board. "Who is the victim, please?" asked the cop.

Muna raised her hand.

From the cop's radio attached to his collar, a voice

crackled, "Suspect in custody. Van on route to precinct seven."

"Would you like to file a report here remotely?" asked the cop. "Use of our synced services is subject to nominal fees and taxes."

"Thank you, Officer," said Muna. She dabbed the handkerchief at her eyes. "Money is no object."

Detective Montgomery pushed open the interview room door, where Bob Landen sat in a chair in front of monitors and microphones. Sweat ran down his temples, despite the air conditioning blasting from the vents.

"I'm Detective Cynthia Montgomery," she said. "I'll be conducting this interview." She checked that the film was rolling by verifying the recording light was on, and checked mics were receiving by blowing into them. They were.

"Am I under arrest?" asked Bob Linden.

Cynthia stepped back to look down at him. "Do you think you should be?"

He frowned. "I'm not answering any questions. I know Muna Sims is trying to make me look like a crazy stalker or something, but I'm not."

"I believe you," she said. "But we'll get to that." She walked in a half circle behind his chair. "My information is that you're in possession of stolen property."

"What?" said Bob. He twisted to try to see her.

"Stolen from United Waste Management Enterprises."

"What?" he said again. "No, no, no. They are my personnel records. I have the legal right to know what's in them."

Cynthia walked back around to stand beside him. "That's true. How do we prove that's what they are, though?"

Bob narrowed his eyes at her. Then he dug a plastic case out of his shirt pocket. "You look at them."

"Are you voluntarily surrendering what's in this case?" she asked.

His scowl deepened.

"It's for the cameras," she said. "I can't take anything personal from you without permission. Unless you're under arrest."

Bob stuck out the plastic case. "Yeah, I'm surrendering or whatever."

She took the case. "Thanks." She bumped open the interview room door with her foot and walked into the room beside it. There, she pried open the small item, removed a flat, silver-colored compound, and then the smooth, brown disc hidden beneath it.

Lamphrey had managed to get the recording device onto Bob Linden's person, like he said he could. Whether it functioned right, or collected any information important to the case, remained to be seen.

◇

Rusty sat in an overly soft office chair. His elbows were propped on the cherrywood desk in front of him. Muna was there, in a matching chair, holding a stack of folders and papers in her lap. Beside her was the litigation lawyer Muna had procured, and whom she'd dubbed "Lil One" because he was young and eager. Rusty assumed she was screwing him.

Across from them sat an entire row of suit-wearers. Two on the end were the investors that put "Enterprises" in United Waste Management. The rest were representatives, lawyers, some titles Rusty had already forgotten. The suit-wearers talked among themselves, while Rusty and Muna waited.

The office walls were panels of glass with automatic shades between, that adjusted their angle with the rising and setting of the sun. Just now, the sun was high over the city, and Rusty could look down through the walls and slats to the coastline and its boardwalk piers. He watched a fisherman baiting shrimp onto a line while gulls dived and swooped to snatch it before it went underwater.

Rusty had already bought his license for fishing for snook from those piers. He'd been searching online for fishing boats and charter boats, too. It had been a few weeks of healing at home, and only a few more would get him ready to haul in mackerel and maybe some spiny lobster, too.

"In conclusion," said a woman in the center of the suits, pulling Rusty's attention back to the room. "We feel it's only right to not just be fair, but to be generous.

We believe you'll agree." The woman slid a piece of paper across the table.

Muna's lawyer reached for the paper, but Muna snatched it, spun it to read it, and frowned. "Generous?" she said. "This is barely the court costs we'd save you by settling. That doesn't even take into consideration the publicity, the OSHA flags, or the stock values after an ugly lawsuit." Muna pushed the paper back across the table. "If that's how you define generous, it's no wonder Rusty hasn't gotten a raise in seven years."

The woman turned her shocked face Muna's lawyer, who sat stone faced. Muna's greatest asset to the proceedings was just being herself; a lawyer worth his exorbitant fee would know it and exploit it. This lawyer did.

The woman then turned to the others, who blustered and shook their heads. They leaned into a discussion like a football huddle, gesturing. Whispering. Eventually, the woman spun in her chair and presented a new piece of paper.

Muna eyed the paper without touching it. She glanced at her lawyer, and back to the paper. "We're almost there." She looked at each of the suits in the eye, one at a time. "Add another zero," she said.

The woman in the middle flinched, but only for a split-second. "Then you'll sign?" she asked.

No one even looked at Rusty.

"We'll sign," Muna said.

The woman opened a notebook. Inside was a flexible keyboard, and she typed into it. A similar notebook inside one of Muna's folders gave a short buzz. Muna opened the folder, eyed the screen, and then showed it under the table to her lawyer, and then Rusty.

It had already been added to their account. Rusty swallowed hard. That was *money*, money, and it would buy a lot of fishing boats.

Unified Reps passed paperwork across the table. Rusty and Muna signed.

Lamphrey paced the hallway in the Cocoa Beach high-rise, peeking in through the smoked glass of the office door each time he passed it. He didn't know why he kept doing that; the conference room where the settlement meeting was taking place was at the back of the office, and he couldn't see that far in.

Detective Montgomery was there, sitting in a cushy, geometrically shaped chair near the wall. She was watching him. "Why do you keep looking?" she asked.

Harper, Rusty's son, hadn't said anything the entire time. He just sat on the floor with a video game in his hands.

"What's taking so long?" asked Lamphrey.

The detective shrugged and closed her eyes. She leaned her head back against the chair's weirdly angled headrest. "Lawyers make everything take longer than it should."

Lamphrey saw a door crack open, and one of the United Waste executives emerged. "Here they come," he said. He stood by the detective, clenching and opening his hands.

She opened one eye. "You look more nervous now than you did while you were waiting," she said.

"I guess I am," he said. There was a lot riding on the next few minutes in all of their lives. One small glitch could ruin everything. He didn't say out loud what he was most nervous about. That Rusty would see dollar signs and change his mind.

The office door opened. Executives and United reps spilled out. They were somber, not chatting. What did that mean? He glanced at the detective, but her eyes were closed.

"Hi, Mr. Flanagan," said Lamphrey, when he spotted the graying man and his handlebar moustache.

"Lamphrey," Mr. Flanagan said as he passed.

Finally, Muna and Rusty and their lawyer appeared in the doorway. Rusty was wearing his new blue suit, just for the occasion, and Lamphrey drew in a breath. The suit broadened Rusty's shoulders and brightened his eyes.

Rusty caught Lamphrey checking him out and gave him a wink. So Rusty hadn't changed his mind.

The detective stood up, finally.

Muna stopped short. "What is *she* doing here?" At first, Muna frowned in anger. Then, she tensed. Lamphrey could swear the temperature in the hallway dropped five degrees.

"Hey, Harper," said Rusty. "Did you give Lamphrey any trouble?"

Lamphrey bent down and tousled Harper's hair. "He's been quiet as a statue."

Harper smiled and looked up from his video game to put his hair back into place.

"Hello, Detective," said Rusty. "Good to see you."

"Likewise," said Detective Montgomery. She approached Rusty, and dropped a smooth, brown disc onto his palm. Muna saw it, and red blotches started filling into her face.

Rusty turned to the lawyer with the cute cleft in his chin. Lamphrey couldn't remember his name.

"Matt? You have the paperwork?" Rusty asked him.

Oh yeah. Matt.

Matt parted the sides of his briefcase, and pulled out a second, zippered file case.

Now Muna turned completely red. "Matt? What the fuck is going on?"

"Language, Mom," said Harper, still staring down at his game.

"Muna," said Rusty, holding open the office door. "We need to talk privately."

"We what?"

Lamphrey could feel the storm brewing. He was actually afraid to let Rusty go in alone with Muna. She was capable of anything once she blasted her hurricane-force winds.

Muna glared at everyone, slowly, and individually. Even Harper. Matt took a step back from the heat of her gaze and loosened his tie.

Then Muna lifted her chin and pranced through

the office door like it was her idea to begin with. Rusty let the door close behind them.

Lamphrey looked at Matt, at Detective Montgomery, and Harper, who had looked up at the sound of the closing door. No one spoke.

Rusty led Muna toward the same conference room they'd just been in. "You're going to tell me what the fuck is going on, right now," she said through clenched teeth.

"Let's go inside," said Rusty.

"I'm not taking another step."

Rusty shrugged, and faced her, "Have it your way. *Moon.*" At that, all the crimson that had collected in her face drained.

Rusty held up the disk that Detective Montgomery had given him. "Recognize this?"

Muna glanced through the office door at the others in the hallway, outside. "Goddammit," she said. She pulled Rusty into the conference room and closed the door.

She didn't speak again, just put her hands on her hips and stared at the disk. Rusty pressed the edge. Out came recorded voices.

"*There was no way to get the control panel to stop communicating with the load arm,*" said Bob's voice. "*The thing was built to launch spaceships, Moon.*"

Then, Muna's voice. "*Well, it doesn't exactly look like*

an accident now, does it?"

Rusty clicked off the recording.

To her credit, Muna remained still. She looked for a long time at Rusty before she finally said, "What do you want?"

"I have divorce papers for you to sign," said Rusty.

"You used my lawyer to draw up your divorce papers," said Muna, her voice flat. Her eyes dark.

"In them," he continued, "Is a quitclaim, which I have already signed, giving you the house. There is also an asset claim which you will sign over to me, relinquishing all settlement money received as a result of litigation concerning my work-related incident."

"Rusty..." she said, quietly. She didn't move, but her eyes were on him. Focused. Her rage was there, seething.

He set the papers on the conference table and pulled a pen from his pocket.

"I can fight you," she said. "I'm entitled to half your--"

Rusty pressed the side of the button again. *"A detective was there when Rusty woke up Wednesday. That bitch is not going to make this easy,"* said Muna's voice.

She uncrossed her arms.

Suddenly, it hit him. There she stood, with a head full of hateful thoughts, and she didn't say any of them. He hadn't ever known a time like this, not in all the years they'd been together. He wished he could press the moment into a photo album.

She took the pen. She stalked to the paperwork, glared at it, and signed, initialed, and signed again.

On second thought, he wanted to keep *that* moment in a photo album.

Cynthia felt a buzz in her pocket. She heard the same buzz from the lawyer's briefcase, and from Mr. Peterson's pocket. She retrieved the flexible netpad Rusty had given her and checked her bank account. A bit of cash for letting him borrow evidence for a few minutes. Her daughter's student loan was compounding daily and taking them both down with it. Ten minutes of rule-breaking was worth it.

The lawyer opened his briefcase, checked his netpad, and then nodded his goodbye. Cynthia hadn't heard him speak so much as a word the whole time, and he didn't say anything then, either.

Mr. Peterson hadn't even glanced at the buzz in his pocket. His eyes were fixed on the door. Then he breathed out and stepped back. He clasped his hands together and gave a little hop. "She signed," he said.

"Signed what?" asked the preteen on the floor. She'd nearly forgotten about him.

"Your mom and dad are divorced, Harper." Mr. Peterson turned to the kid. "How do you feel about that?"

"Are you going to be my stepdad?" Harper asked.

"Well, how would you feel about *that*?"

Harper shrugged. "Every kid in my class has a step-parent. They think it's weird I don't."

The office door opened. Mrs. Sims was so pale and drooping, at first Cynthia thought Rusty had finally lost his temper and slugged her.

He walked her over to Cynthia. "She's all yours, Detective." He dropped the brown disk into Cynthia's hand.

Mrs. Sims' eyes went large. "Wait. Wait!"

"Come on, Mrs. Sims," said Cynthia, taking the woman by her wrists. "Let's do the rest of this away from the kid."

"But I signed! I thought if I signed, Rusty wouldn't... oh, god. Wait," said Mrs. Sims, as Cynthia pushed her along.

"Away from your kid," said Cynthia again.

Rusty watched Muna and the detective disappear into a stairwell. Lamphrey took Rusty's hand, and watched them, too.

Harper stood up and started to follow the women. "Where's Mom going?" he asked.

Lamphrey caught Harper by the arm. "Let's give them a minute."

"Where's she going?" Harper asked again.

"We're going to talk about that at lunch," answered Lamphrey. "Things will be confusing for a while, but it's all going to be okay."

Rusty released a long breath. He gave Lamphrey's hand a squeeze.

Lamphrey turned his head and smiled.

"I want to buy a fishing boat," Rusty said.

The Monster

Accursed creator! Why did you form a monster so hideous that even you turned from me in disgust? God, in pity, made man beautiful and alluring, after his own image; but my form is a filthy type of yours, more horrid even from the very resemblance. Satan had his companions, fellow devils, to admire and encourage him, but I am solitary and abhorred.

— *Mary Shelley's "Frankenstein"*

I woke up with my toes so cold I thought I'd lost the blanket. I patted the bed. There was my thin, over-patched blanket stretched across me where it should be. I peered at the fireplace. The fire had gone out, but that wasn't unusual. My husband, Heinrich, had always been the one to keep a roaring fire glowing until morning.

After all these years I still couldn't manage it myself.

The wind blasted against my window. I held my hand to the pane of glass while it rattled and threatened to come loose. There used to be more sunlight on my bed in the morning. There used to be more sunlight in the entire hut, but over time, as I'd lost a window to the wind, or to children throwing rocks, I'd replaced it with wood. Glass was a luxury shipped in from Hamburg, and I had enough trouble just keeping my larder stocked. I couldn't afford the sun anymore.

I stared across the room, trying to think of a reason to get up. The best I had was if I laid still much longer, I might freeze solid to my straw mattress. I pushed off my bed and shuffled in the dark, fully dressed in layers of flannel, toward the fireplace. Only when I touched the lid of the woodbin did I remember it was empty. My woodpile outside was gone, too.

I groaned. I had already scavenged the wood in the trees around my hut, and all that was left was too green. I considered a trek across the field to the De Lacey farm to ask for wood. In the last year since the De Laceys became my neighbors, they had occasionally been kind, but I didn't trust how long that might last. Any day their kindness might run out.

I had no choice. I grabbed my last jar of berry curd from the larder. The blind De Lacey father loved my berry curd. I wrapped my blanket around me like a cloak, slipped on my wooden clogs, and began the walk across my frostbitten field of dying turnips.

The cold air stung each time I breathed, and by the

time I reached the back steps of my neighbor's home, my lungs felt shriveled. I paused to collect, and to make sure my blanket was appropriately covering my face. Behind me, I heard young Felix De Lacey's voice. "Is that you, Agatha?"

I turned, bowing my face low. "No, forgive me. It is your neighbor, Leisl."

I couldn't see his reaction, but I could feel it. He tensed and eased back a step.

"I haven't yet repaired my axe, and have no wood. I've brought your father some berry curd, if you'll allow me a few sticks of kindling."

Next came Agatha's voice from the porch. "Of course you can have some wood, poor thing. I'm afraid this winter frost has snuck up on all of us. We're quite unprepared, ourselves."

I set the jar on a step so neither De Lacey would have to reach toward me. "You're too kind."

"Our whole crop of turnips is stuck in the frozen ground, and we can't dig them out, though we've tried," said Agatha. "I was just speaking to Father about it. We don't know how we're going to manage without this year's crop."

"My field is the same. I haven't managed to harvest a one," I said. I didn't tell her that I'd also just given them the last of my food.

"Here's your wood, then," said Felix. He dropped a stack to the ground, and I bent to retrieve it.

Agatha whispered behind me. "Maybe you should help her carry it."

"Are you mad? I'm not going over there."

"I'll just be on my way," I said, struggling to manage the heavy load of wood.

"Do you think she's really a witch?" Agatha asked.

"Yes. Did you see her hands?"

"Didn't the villagers say something about a fire?"

"The barn. She and her husband went in, but only she survived. It turned her, they said."

Agatha and her brother had forgotten to whisper, and I was halfway across my field before their voices finally died away. I thought I'd become accustomed to whispers and accusations, but something in the young man's voice affected me. I felt tears stir where tears hadn't been stirred in years.

I veered around my tiny home toward the burned skeleton of my barn. Charred timbers stuck out like demon arms from a mass of melted leather and wood. An eerie feeling crept up my back as it usually did, because I knew Heinrich's body was still a part of that mass somewhere. He'd been trapped inside. There had been nothing left of him to retrieve.

I tried. God knows I tried. I'd stayed and fought and tugged at Heinrich's arms until I thought I'd be swallowed by the fire, and nearly was. His sleeve had torn away, and I'd fallen out onto the snow, my dress and hair smoking. After that, time became a blur of pain and nausea and peeling skin, and only several weeks later did I realize I would survive after all. It was about the same time that I'd realized Heinrich was gone forever, I'd been left to fend for myself, and no one, not a single soul from the village, ever came to help.

I suppose the fire did turn me. Not into the witch young De Lacey accused me of being, but into someone else. Someone just as dark. Maybe I'd been cursed to exist in this disfigured body because it so accurately portrayed what had become of my soul. I leaned my forehead to the wood in my arms and cried.

A stick snapped somewhere to my right. I sucked in my tears, nearly choking, and listened. There were no more sounds, but I sensed someone. Years of being stared at had honed my skills of feeling watched. I didn't give the visitor any time to gather up stones. I ran to my door, dropping planks of wood that I didn't have time to worry about. I pushed my door open with my shoulder, let the rest of the wood tumble to the floor, and slid the bolt.

A shadow passed the small pane of glass near my bed. No yelling. No jeering laughter. Several minutes went by before I gathered the courage to loosen the bolt and peer outside. There, near my footprints in the frost, were the seven planks of wood I'd dropped. Neatly stacked.

The next day I awoke again with cold toes. I'd already burned through the De Lacey's wood from yesterday and had nothing left to barter with for more. The village blacksmith wouldn't speak to me, let alone extend credit to repair my axe. I'd have to try again myself, though I hadn't yet come up with a solution that kept the blade intact. I began to wonder, for the first time, if this might be the winter to do me in. A part of me hoped it would be.

I wrapped my blanket around myself and stepped outside. I gasped. I blinked, unable to believe what I was seeing. There, against my house, was a pile of firewood stacked higher than my head. My axe was propped beside the wood, gleaming in a shaft of sun, the handle repaired.

I raced across my field in my wool stockings, forgetting my clogs. As I got closer to the De Lacey's, I heard the rattle of crates being pushed onto a wooden cart, and the whinny of a horse. "Hello!" I called.

Agatha came to meet me. I made sure my blanket covered my face before I spoke again. "I've just come to thank your brother for the wood this morning."

"You thanked us yesterday, there's no need for you brave the frost again so soon. And without your shoes, poor thing," said Agatha. "But you're here, so come look! Oh, you won't believe such a wonderful thing."

She was surely excited, because she touched my arm and urged me toward her house. Such a pretty house, too, with a freshly thatched roof and bright windows. I hadn't noticed before. It was twice the size of mine, with a little storage hovel around back.

"Look! Do you see the cart so full of turnips? We're going into the village now, and what a spree we'll have!" Agatha's voice squeaked with emotion. "We don't even know how they got plowed up, we just found them this morning!"

"Someone dug up your turnips for you?" I turned slowly, searching the trees around our adjacent fields. "Someone chopped me such a wall of wood I may be warm all winter."

"Oh?" Agatha asked, following my searching eyes with her own. "Maybe we have the same secret helper."

Someone with strength enough to dig out turnips from frozen ground, and still manage to chop a forest of wood in one night? "Whoever it was, I wish I could thank him in person," I said, raising my voice a little, just in case the secret helper was watching. I had the feeling he was.

"Maybe next he'll plow your turnips, too." Agatha smiled. Then she spun around and climbed onto the horse cart.

I nodded but doubted it very much; I couldn't expect two acts of kindness from a stranger. Even so, all the way home I had an uncomfortable flutter in my gut, and when I again saw the stacked wood, I had to press my hand to my stomach to keep it from turning an actual flip in hope. Not so much for the turnips, but for something more. Something I couldn't bring myself to form a thought around.

It was more likely, anyway, that the whole thing was really some sort of cruel farce. Maybe, come morning, the firewood would be gone again. Well, if that's what someone intended, I would get the better of that!

I spent the day hauling as much wood inside as I could manage. Load after load, I filled the woodbin and stacked piles around the fireplace, and even crammed some under my bed.

That night I fell into bed hungry and exhausted. I tried to listen for sounds outside, but before I could recognize anything new, it was morning again.

I lay in bed waiting. I kept trying to convince myself that today would be just another day. With or without firewood, or with or without turnips, life would go on as it always had. Finally, I set my feet on my floor and crept to the door. I peered outside.

Turnips! They were the first things I saw. I spotted them piled at the corner of my house, spilling down across the frozen yard. Oh, and larger than I remembered them being last year, and creamy yellow and red and perfect. I couldn't help myself. I ran out to them and turned one over and over in my hand, and laughed, right out loud. This winter wouldn't do me in, after all.

My first task would be to set a pot of steaming turnip stew over the fire to cook. Next, I would steel myself for a trip into town. I despised facing the village. The merchants pointed and women waved their hands as though warding off some hex I was putting on them just by trying to buy their vegetables. I would keep my visit short and stealthy, gathering only necessities, but I would have food in the larder. I had wood for a winter. I thought I just might cry again.

◇

My shopping trip went easier than I'd expected. Only three women shook their fists at me, and I managed to bring home a crate full of carrots, flour, milk, and more. I felt as victorious as if I'd climbed Der Watzmann itself.

I'd only just put a spoon to my lips to taste my soup, and hadn't unpacked yet from my trip, when there came a furious pounding at my door. Startled, I dropped the spoon. "Who's there?" I called.

"It's Agatha! Hurry!"

I covered myself and opened the door a little.

"I shouldn't have taken the time, but had to warn you, poor thing. You won't believe what's happened." Agatha's face was pink with fright. "With all the talk in town of a monster in these parts...and I thought they were exaggerating..."

"What's happened?"

"Felix and I came in from chores to find him! Right in our house, frightening our father! We shooed him out, of course, risking our very lives. He was a mountain of a creature. Felix had to beat at him with the fire poker to get him to go."

"To get who to go? Who was in your house?"

"The monster!" Agatha put a hand to her forehead. "He was so hideous. I'll never forget his yellow face and his eyes...so like death..."

"What did he do?"

"He didn't have a chance to do anything, thank God and the saints. I'm sure we would have all been victims if we hadn't thought so quickly. I only came to warn you." She turned. "You won't see us anymore, we aren't staying. It isn't safe for you, poor thing." She scurried across the field.

I stared after her, trying to make sense out of what she'd said. I hadn't heard any talk of monsters, except the insults meant for me. I poured hot soup into a mug and sipped at it, pacing.

Then, I don't know what drove me out the door and across the field toward the De Laceys', wrapped in a blanket, my soup mug still in hand. The whole way there, my heart clawed inside me to get back home.

Agatha wasn't exaggerating; the whole family was already gone. The back door was ajar, and I peeked in to see they'd left nothing behind. Ashes dirtied the firebox, and wind whistled eerily down the chimney, scattering them. It felt colder inside than outside.

I crept around the house, looking for footprints. I found a few, frozen hard into the ground, but they could have been anyone's. One particularly large print stood out near the door of the hovel, and I poked at the door to see if it was latched. It wasn't. I pulled it open.

Inside was dark like my house, but for the few bars of gray sunshine leaking through the slats. There was a stench much like when Heinrich would return from hunting and hadn't bathed for days. One corner had a pile of straw. I knelt to pass my hand over it. It was cold, but my fingers brushed something solid. I set down my mug and cleared some straw to find a small leather book. No, three books, stacked together. The top book was named "Paradise Lost." Some papers were spread out near the far wall, as though they'd recently been read.

I heard heavy steps approach, so I scrambled to cover the books. I peered outside. A large mass passed by, and I stared after it, so struck by its size that I took several moments to realize it was a man. He went out of my view again, but I heard him lumber up the steps of the De Lacey home and pause. A wail broke out. A flock of black birds screeched and bolted for the sky.

I would have to pass right behind him to cross to my field. I crept out of the hovel, trying to be silent. He wailed again. It was such a grief-stricken sound, like a moan, really, that it stopped my heart. It stopped my feet. I slowly peered over my shoulder to find him watching me. I couldn't see his face, because he was covered, like me, but I felt his eyes.

He was afraid of me.

He lumbered toward the trees, his howl trailing behind him.

My blood turned as cold as my feet. I knew then why I'd come looking for the monster. I'd dared to hope he really did exist, and that he'd be one—just one—to understand. "I'm not a witch!" I called. He either didn't hear me, or didn't believe me. "I'm not a witch," I said under my breath. He ran anyway. I watched him disappear into the trees.

Snow sprinkled from the darkening sky. It gathered on the tops of my clogs, clung to the edge of my blanket. I stared at it, feeling it heavy like clotted dirt; as though I was being buried alive.

No, not alive. Walking and breathing, yes, but in a body meant for the grave. Maybe that's what everyone sensed about me. Maybe they all knew somehow that the fire was meant for both Heinrich and me, and without meaning to, I'd cheated it. I shouldn't have tried to pull Heinrich from the fire; I should have jumped into it. If I'd known how dead I was going to be anyway, I would have.

"I'm not a witch!" I heard myself scream. I ran for my house. My blanket fell off somewhere between here and there, but I didn't care anymore. I didn't care if I had wood for the winter, or food in my larder. In fact, I hated that I did.

I demolished the wall of wood outside. I threw each piece as far as I could manage, then ran inside to clear out the piles and piles off it that I'd spent yesterday so carefully stacking. Out into the falling snow it went, clattering onto the frozen ground. "Get out!" I shrieked, as though it could hear me.

Next went the flour and bacon and all the things I'd just brought back from the village. Dead people didn't need food, and I wasn't going to pretend that I was alive anymore. I was still trying to scream and rant, but my throat was sore and my words weren't making sense. I just wailed out into the sky each time I opened the door and sent another bundle flying.

Finally, there was nothing left to throw out. I dropped onto my bed, trembling from rage. Then, as my rage trickled away, I trembled from cold. I was glad it was so cold. I would probably freeze to death before I could starve to death, and the faster my relief, the better. I refused to allow tears.

I awoke with warm toes. I wiggled them. I wiggled my fingers. They were warm, too. I was surprised. I didn't think death would feel so warm. I opened my eyes.

Fire blazed in the hearth. Orange light reflected off the black iron of my old, familiar bed. Wind rattled my last glass windowpane. I thought I smelled warm turnip stew.

I sat up, almost failing to recognize my own hut in the soothing glow of fire. I couldn't figure out if this was my afterlife, or just some in-between stop on the way. I was still trying to make sense of it when I spotted my wooden mug on the seat of my rocking chair.

I walked toward the chair. My mug was perched atop my wool blanket, which was neatly folded and still damp from being left in the snow. And hadn't I accidentally left my mug in the De Lacey hovel?

Then movement caught my eye. A massive form was hunched beneath a cloak, crouching near the door. I was frightened of many things all at once, but the most urgent was that I'd been *seen*. I gasped, scrambling to throw my blanket around my head and shoulders. My mug clattered to the floor.

"Don't fear," came a rumble of a voice. The form stood and reached for the door. "I only meant to…I was…"

I recognized him then. He was the stranger from last night. I must have been watching him with curious eyes, because he tilted his head beneath his shadowy hood. I looked away.

From the corner of my eye, I saw his shoulders were drawn tight, and he kept his hand on the door, ready to bolt. I didn't know what to say, and, apparently, neither did he, so we both listened to the crackle of the fire for a long time.

"Thank you," I finally said, though I was still wishing he'd left me alone to die.

"Don't fear me," he said again, his voice soft.

"I don't."

"But you hide." He pointed a thick finger at my blanket.

I nodded. "So do you."

He touched the edge of his hood. "I must."

"Why?"

He sighed then; his breath laced with grief. "What's your name?" I asked.

He sighed again. "No name."

"You don't remember?"

He turned away and poked at the door handle. "I only meant to warm you. With fire. And to watch until you were safe."

"Why?" I asked.

He opened the door.

"Don't go," I whispered, afraid he might hear me. Afraid he might not.

Cold air crept across my feet as the stranger stared

out into the dreary morning. "I heard your sounds. From your throat. In the trees I heard you and my heart knew those sounds. I thought you called me."

"Then why won't you stay?"

"You will see me. You will be afraid of me."

"You're afraid of me because you've seen me."

He turned to face me.

"That's really why you won't stay," I said, my bitterness returning, leaking into my voice. "You think I'm a witch, like everyone else, because I'm hideous. It's easy for you to do nice things like chop my wood and make me a fire, as long as you don't have to look at me, but you can't bear to talk to me or treat me like an actual—"

He pulled back his hood to expose his face, and my words caught. His dark eyes flashed with an anger that tightened my throat. Then I saw the scars. One traveled down his cheek to his neck. One drew his upper lip into a sneer. Another disappeared under the collar of his cloak. His skin was the faint yellow of a peeled onion, but his hair was thick and black and puddled into the hood against his back. It looked soft.

"What happened?" I asked.

He looked away. "I was made this way."

"You mean you were born that way?"

"No," he said.

I took a step toward him. "May I touch your hair?"

His face darted toward me, and his eyes narrowed. Then he nodded once.

I drew my fingers down the black strands, like silk

beneath my touch. I would have liked to do it again, but he was still staring intently at me, and I grew self-conscious. I gripped the blanket beneath my chin.

"You are not afraid?" he asked.

I shook my head.

"I would not hurt you," he said.

"I believe you."

His shoulders loosened. "You would... be my friend?"

I hesitated. Not because I didn't want his friendship, but because I'd forgotten exactly what that meant. "Yes," I finally said.

His features brightened. He smiled, his lips peeling away from white teeth. His left cheek, the one without the scar, had a dimple. Then his smile faded. "But you hide."

He reached for my blanket, but I stepped away from his touch. He frowned.

"I can't," I said.

"But I saw you. There." He pointed toward my bed. "Sleeping."

"You did?" My heart dropped. I'd hoped it had been too dark.

"Yes. Your face is..." He trailed off, his brow wrinkling as he searched for the right word.

"Hideous," I said.

He shook his head.

"Ugly."

He shook his head again. "No." He drew a small book from inside his cloak and held it with thick and knobby fingers. I recognized it from the hovel.

"Paradise Lost," I said. "Johannes Miltoni."

He nodded. He watched me for a time. Then he opened the book and drew his finger down a page. He pulled in a breath. "At once delight and horror on us seize, Thou singst with so much gravity and ease; And above humane flight dost soar aloft, with plume so strong, so equal, and so soft."

I wasn't sure what he meant, so I didn't speak.

"You are a bird," he said. "You fly higher than most, and you see more than they can."

"A wounded bird, maybe," I said, tears welling.

"Yes. But strong. Beautiful."

"What?"

"Beautiful," he repeated.

This time, when he reached for my blanket, I let him take it. I watched his face, bracing for his reaction. He drew in a sharp breath. "Your eyes. They match the sky."

I waited for the pounding of my heart to subside. It didn't. I watched his distorted mouth, wondering what it would feel like to kiss it.

"I'm no witch," I said then.

"No." He shook his head. "I'm no monster."

We smiled.

Frontier Hero

It's a dusty road in a dusty town between two dusty hills of Oklahoma territory. The sun is sharp like a rattlesnake bite, stinging your eyes, and glinting hard off the tin roof of the old watering hole townsfolk call "The Old Watering Hole."

In the distance, Outlaw Bart stands bow-legged and tense, his hand near his sidearm, fingers twitchy.

A tumbleweed rolls across the dirt road.

"*I ain't looking for trouble, Sheriff," says Outlaw Bart. "I'm just passing through."*

You, [say name into device], *step forward in your cowboy boots, spurs jangling. Your sheriff badge shines into Bart's eyes. Your thumbs are hooked into your gun belt, with a hand-me-down revolver holster worn by your daddy, and his daddy before him.*

"Come quietly," you say, "We'll avoid all that."

Wind blows. Outlaw Bart's WANTED poster rattles against the wood siding of The Old Watering Hole.

Bart's fingers begin reaching toward his gun. "I ain't the kind to come quietly."

"Then you got some trouble," you say.

Bart draws. A shot rings out. Bart drops to the dust.

You slide your gun into your holster. Narrow your eyes.

Jezebel, the farmer's daughter, runs to you, her blonde braids like twisted gold. "You did it, Sheriff! That mean ol' snake of an outlaw can rot where he lays."

You push up your hat with one finger. "Just doing my job, ma'am," you say. "Just doing my job."

Jezebel smiles and looks up at you through her lashes. "Can I see your gun, Sheriff? I ain't never seen a man's gun up close."

You smile, too, and lay your gun in her hands. "Call me Donald," you say.

She giggles. "All right. Donald."

"Donald." Lydia Aimes shook her husband's shoulders where he was stretched out on his threadbare recliner. She knocked on the virtual reality goggles over his eyes. "Donald! Were you up all night again?"

He still made no movement or reply, so she put her hands on either side of the goggles and tried to wiggle them loose.

Donald's hands shot up and grabbed her around her wrists. "Lydia! For Chrissakes!" He sat up, then, his recliner sliding upright, and he unfastened the goggles from electrodes across his forehead. "Are you trying to give me a stroke?"

"Mr. Roberts called."

"I have to disconnect internally. You understand? Or else brain damage."

Lydia watched him tug the electrodes from his skin, leaving behind small patches of glue. It seemed like those spots were a little cleaner than the rest of his face, or maybe it was just reddened contrast to his sooty pallor; the same lackluster hue of everyone's skin these days, no matter the race, Black, White, Asian, Latinx. The air was turning everyone gray, especially her patients at the clinic.

Donald pushed to his feet and blinked at the brightness through the window. "Jesus, what time is it?"

"Almost nine."

"Jesus," Donald said again. He pressed his rumpled shirt into the waist of his slacks and rushed toward the door.

"I told him you'd left already. But that's the third time this week!"

"Call you later." Donald smoothed down his thinning hair with one hand and opened the front door with his other.

"And that's the same shirt you wore-"

The door banged shut.

Lydia scowled after him. Then she bent to run her hands along the recliner seams, searching for the game goggles. There was nothing but potato chips and vanilla wafer crumbs in the recliner's cushions. She scowled again at the door.

Donald set his Vee Real goggles on the bottom shelf of his locker and stepped into his white Renews-It coverall. He'd managed to sneak past the front office without drawing attention and had already checked the call log. He was hoping to slip back out without crossing paths with his supervisor at all.

He was just pinning his name-and-certification badge on his chest when he heard the rustling approach of a cheap suit.

"Mr. Aimes," said Mr. Roberts. Donald hated when his supervisor called him that. It wasn't meant respectfully. "I needed you out on that call a half hour ago."

"I'm heading into town now," said Donald. He tucked his Vee Real goggles beneath his arm and closed his locker door.

"Take Brian with you."

Donald just nodded without looking. He tried to hurry, without appearing to hurry, toward the locker room's exit.

"And you're going to work through lunch!" Mr. Roberts called.

On the other side of the double doors, he nearly collided with Brian. Brian had pulled the hood of his coverall around his head and was tying it under his chin.

"What's the rush?" Brian asked. "Seen a ghost?"

"Unfortunately," said Donald. He followed Brian in pulling his hood up and over his head to fasten it into place.

Brian smiled, watching him. "Man, you *are* the ghost."

Donald chuckled, because it was true. When Brian wore his coverall, the stark white of it made Brian's dark skin even darker, but somehow the same material made Donald's white skin go even paler; mottled and opaque like cheap paper. Most days, he felt like cheap paper. Balled up and left in the trash.

"Let's go," said Brian. He held up the truck keys.

They left through the employee exit and went across the Renews-It lot toward truck 003. Donald peered at the cloudy PTFE chemical tank affixed to the bed. "Looks low."

"We'll drop it off for a refill after the call," said Brian.

Brian drove them out of the lot, and across the expanse of muddy grass and gravel that opened out onto a throughway toward town. The nearest neighborhoods looked convincingly normal, with trees arching over the rooftops, freshly painted concrete siding, and irrigated lawns. But Donald could see beyond the first glance, to the yellowed edges of leaves, the layers of crackle beneath the paint, and the lawns turned limp and brown.

The people in those houses were probably pretending their lives were normal, too. Just working and shopping, carousing and resting as always. Still hearing the Intergovernmental Science warnings. Still breathing poisoned air. Still ignoring it all.

But as the truck crossed over the center of town and onto Blair Street, the devastation was too obvious to pretend. These streets had always been grimy and graffiti-filled, but now what was left of the brick and concrete had crumbled into lumpy ruins. Even the trees were bent and blackened. Stringy vines, leafless but stubborn, engulfed entire buildings. Only the occasional peek at exposed stairways or overturned furniture through broken windows gave any hint that these, too, were once homes.

The truck's navigation beeped at them to turn right in one mile.

Brian and Donald exchanged a look. "One mile?" said Brian.

Donald opened the gas mask compartment of the dashboard and passed one to Brian. "You sure the address is right?" he asked.

"Far as I know," said Brian.

Brian followed the navigation and eventually turned right, past billboards that once read WARNING and EVAC ZONE, but were now peeling and singed as though from invisible fire.

Then the navigation system beeped that they had reached their destination. Brian and Donald looked around at the flat, gray remains of pavement and concrete. Donald wasn't quite sure what destination the truck was referring to.

Then, Donald spotted movement within a vine-covered blob. The movement pushed the foliage aside just enough that he could see a door. Then he saw a face, peering out around the door. "You gotta be kidding me," he said.

"Is that a person?" Brian asked, his voice soft. He slid his gas mask over his head.

Donald put on his, too, and tightened the straps extra firm. Then he opened the truck door.

Outside, he unlatched a side panel on the truck, and pulled out the long, thin hoses that would spray the decontamination compound from the PTFE container.

He saw Brian come around the side of the truck, holding a Geiger counter. It was already clicking.

They walked to the door, and to the bent and wrinkled woman who tilted her head to look up at them. Donald thought she might be elderly, but she couldn't have survived long enough in this part of town to *become* old.

"Ma'am, you should have been evacuated from here a long time ago," said Brian.

"They told us to leave," she said. "I've got nowhere to go."

"It was you who called in a cleanup?" asked Donald. The woman nodded.

Brian checked his Geiger, looked at Donald, and shook his head.

"Have you checked your levels latcly?" Donald asked the woman.

"The inserts, they're so expensive," she said.

Brian looked at the truck, and then at Donald, and

at the hoses in Donald's hands. "Then how are you able to pay for—"

Donald shoved the hoses into Brian's hand and took the Geiger. "Just give the lady what she wants. Don't skimp."

Brian hesitated, but then began a walk around what was left of the building to begin his sweep.

Donald dug down into a zippered pocket of his coverall and retrieved a cartridge of insertable treatment vials. ITVs, or inserts, some called them. Injectable if you had the accompanying click-pen; drinkable if you didn't. And if you could stand the taste of raw monkey ass.

"Take these for now," said Donald. "When they run out, visit the clinic on Poplar."

"I've tried there. I just can't stand in line all those hours," said the woman.

"You go right inside. Ask for Lydia."

The woman studied his face, and then smiled and reached out to accept the inserts.

"You'll remember who to ask for?" said Donald.

"I'll remember," said the woman. "Lydia."

Lydia walked through the dismal waiting room of the Poplar Street Clinic, between parents with crying children, and children with coughing parents. People sat in every available seat. She'd already looted the storage room for folding chairs and wooden crates, and those were occupied, too. More patients stood in a line that went around the back walls and out the clinic door.

She tried to remember if the clinic had ever had a slow day in her five years working there. She couldn't recall one. She also couldn't recall if the carpet had ever been cleaned or had ever smelled like anything other than mildew and hopelessness.

She adjusted her mask to more fully cover her nose and continued on. She offered patients forms and pencils from the pockets on her scrubs, encouraging them and speaking softly.

A hand with the oozing skin of chem burns clutched at the hem of her top. "Please," croaked the man in a folding chair, his eyes red and watering.

"Only a few more minutes now," she said. "Do you have your form?"

The man held up a sheet of paper.

"And your I.D.?"

The man patted his shirt pocket and nodded.

"Good. That will speed things up." She touched the man on his shoulder and tried to smile into his eyes. "You'll feel better soon," she said.

She was lying, of course. She didn't know which was worse anymore; facing the daily hordes of the sick and dying, or the constant breaking of promises she made to them.

She weaved her way back toward the office side of the partition, and, suddenly dizzy, put out her hand to brace herself against the particle board wall.

A physician's assistant, Paula, spotted her, and

paused. "Lydia? You need a break?"

She shook her head. "I skipped breakfast. I'm fine."

Paula didn't seem convinced, but moved off anyway, too busy to linger for conversation.

"You're Lydia?" asked a voice.

Lydia turned to find a young mother, maybe in her twenties, wearing a sweatshirt too big, and stretch pants too small. She balanced a child on her hip. The mother's nose was bleeding.

"I was told I could ask you about treatment," said the mother.

"Told by whom?"

"His name was Donald."

Lydia pulled a tissue from the pocket of her scrubs and pressed it to the mother's nosebleed. "Pinch your fingers tight right here."

The mother tried to, with her free arm, but struggled to hold the baby while she did. Lydia grabbed the child before it slipped.

"I'm not asking for me," said the mother. "Just my baby."

Lydia hoisted the toddler onto her own hip and looked down at the child. A girl, with tiny braids held by pipe cleaners. A trickle of blood appeared in the girl's nostril.

"Okay," she said quietly. "Go wait at the back, and I'll—"

"Hey!" shouted a man's voice. That man stood, holding a baseball cap, and pointed it at the mother. "She didn't wait her turn!"

Others spun in their chairs. Some stared in surprise. Others stood, too, and began to speak to each other, angry.

"Sir," said Lydia. "If you could please remain calm-"

"I've been here three hours!" the man shouted.

"I understand, but she's giving up her place for her daughter. I'm not treating the woman, just the child."

"My baby needs treatment," said another woman, standing. She held an infant, wrapped in a disheveled quilt. "Will you take her?" she asked.

More parents stood, pushing their children forward, elbowing to make space. Voices called out, trying to be heard, the noise of it growing louder.

Lydia motioned to the woman with the infant to come forward.

Paula was there, standing beside Lydia. She shook her head. "You can't do this. Dr. Rivers is already watching you."

Lydia handed the toddler to Paula. Then, when the second mother reached them, she took the infant in the quilt.

"I promise, I'll go to the back of the line." The woman turned, and both mothers began making their way back into the angry throng, pushing at people with their shoulders, trying to go outside.

Lydia regarded Paula a moment, and then turned to the crowd, shouting over the din, "Listen!"

Shouting quieted. Faces turned.

"Right now, today only," said Lydia. "I'll take every child in this line, here and now. But I need volunteers to give up their places…"

Almost every hand in the room raised.

"I don't have a child," called a young man, who stood, his hand raised, too. "But my father is very sick, and I'll give up my place for him." The young man's hand rested on the shoulder of an old man Lydia recognized; the one with chem burns on his hands.

Lydia hesitated, reading the crowd, but they were busy jostling to move their children forward. They were hugging their young ones, kissing their cheeks, murmuring that things were going to be all right.

Lydia nodded at the young man, and he helped his father stand, and braced him as he made his way forward. Lydia, still holding the infant, turned to herd the crowd of youth collecting around her. She held the wiggling infant against her chest. "Be sure to give them your forms," she said to the parents.

As she and Paula led the children toward the treatment rooms, she felt a touch on her shoulder.

"Thank you," said the father, his voice tight with emotion.

Lydia smiled. "Thank your son," she said, and then looked down at the infant in her arms. She might get to keep some promises today.

In the distance, Outlaw Bart stands bow-legged and tense, his hand near his sidearm, fingers twitchy.
A tumbleweed rolls across the dirt road.

"I ain't looking for trouble, Sheriff. Deputy." says Outlaw Bart. "I'm just passing through."

You both step forward in your cowboy boots, spurs jangling. Sheriff Donald's badge shines into Bart's eyes, and Deputy Brian's badge glints in a ray of hot sun. Your thumbs are hooked into your gun belts, with hand-me-down revolver holsters worn by your daddies, and their daddies before them.

"Come quietly," says Sheriff Donald. "We'll avoid all that."

Wind blows. Outlaw Bart's WANTED poster rattles against the wood siding of The Old Watering Hole.

Bart grabs Jezebel, the farmer's daughter, from the crowd and presses a gun to her neck. "I ain't the kind to come quietly," says Bart.

Jezebel gasps.

"Looks like we got us some trouble, Sheriff," says Deputy Brian.

Sheriff Donald nods. "You know what to do."

A three-way glare. Eyes narrow. A shot rings out. Bart stumbles back a step, hit in the shoulder. Jezebel runs to the arms of her father.

Sheriff Donald dives behind a watering trough for cover. Deputy Brian runs and slides behind a stack of barrels on the steps of The Old Watering Hole.

Bart aims with his good arm, piercing a hole in the brim of Deputy Brian's cowboy hat.

"Now you done it," says Deputy Brian. He peers around a barrel, aiming his gun.

Sheriff Donald squeezes the trigger of his revolver.

Bart stumbles again, hit in the other shoulder.
A distant buzzer sounds.

In the dashboard of the Renews-It truck cab, an alarm sounded, signaling the end of lunch break. Brian, in the front seat, unhooked his VisVisor game goggles from over his ears. "Aw, man. I hardly got a shot off." He punched the alarm to silence it.

"You got to be quick, Brian," said Donald, who sat beside him with a wrapped sandwich in his lap. He unlatched his goggles from his forehead electrodes.

Brian didn't have any electrodes to remove. "I think there was a delay. It didn't crossplay right."

Donald chuckled. "Keep making excuses. Go ahead."

Brian watched Donald collect his electrodes and place them in the storage flap on the Vee Real headset. "You and I make the same money. How do you afford these kinds of upgrades?" he asked.

Donald just shrugged.

"And VisVisor and Vee Real aren't even supposed to be compatible."

"I know a guy," said Donald.

Brian stared. "Did I just play a bootleg?"

"I didn't say that."

"Man, bootlegging is some serious shit," said Brian. "All up in the brainpan. I heard they've got viruses that'll make you pee yourself."

"Do I look sick?"

Brian reached for Donald's Vee Real and turned

it over in his hands. "Some of that Jezebel action's probably worth it. I level up, I'll get me some of that." He backhanded Donald's arm. "Every time's the first time, right?"

"I wouldn't know," said Donald. He took his Vee Real from Brian and wrapped it in its protective plexiglass.

"What?" Brian laughed. "You've never taken her around back to *show her your gun?* All this time on level 10?"

"I'm a married man, partner."

"Not in the game," said Brian. "It's not like it's real, man."

Donald unfolded his sandwich from its paper.

"Come on," said Brian. "Tell me you haven't thought about it."

Donald took a bite of his liverwurst on rye and chewed silently, regarding Brian.

Brian reached for his paper lunch bag on the cab floor. "Everyone's thought about it," he said. "Hell, everyone does it." He unwrapped his sandwich and lifted a slice of sourdough to peek under it. "Aw, lettuce again. Why they gotta keep putting green shit on my roast beef?" He peeled the soggy lettuce from the sandwich innards and laid it on the wrapper. "But yeah," he continued, "Everyone does it. It's what upgrades are all about, what people keep spending hard-earned credits for. What's the point in meds, man?" He held out his sandwich. "Why eat?" He took a large bite of his sandwich, chewing and talking around the bread in his mouth. "We got drinking, and we got game."

"*I* got game," said Donald. "*You* can't hit the broad side of a barn."

"Fuck you say?" said Brian. "Meet me in Starfield one of these days, man, I'll show you shooting. With real modern weapons, not this cowboy shit."

"All I'm hearing is 'I'm a wuss, I can't shoot'."

"Oh, you're on," said Brian.

Donald re-wrapped his sandwich. "Let's go then. Right now."

"But lunch break's over. And you were supposed to work through it, Mr. Roberts—"

"Fuck him." Donald opened the cover of his Vee Real.

Brian bit off another helping of sandwich, then set it down. "Getting me some of that Jezebel," he said. He slid his VisVisor over his head. "Watch and learn."

At dinner that evening, Lydia sat at the table in the kitchen, in front of the window. She stared outside as the evening sky took on a green-yellow cast, turning their drooping willow trees into drapery-like skirts of fancy ballgowns. It was the only fragment of beauty, for a few brief minutes every day, that their poisoned world had to offer.

She mindlessly stirred at her dinner plate, pushing boiled rice and hydroponic zucchini into little molehills, her gaze on the willow trees. Then she looked over her shoulder at the living room, and at Donald, laid out in his recliner wearing his goggles.

By the time she looked back out the window, the ballgowns had again turned to listless willow branches. She stood, scraped her plate into the trash bin, and rinsed it in the sink.

Donald hadn't even touched his food. She wrapped his plate with foil and slid it into the refrigerator. Then she walked to him, pulled the couch's ottoman over to his recliner, and sat beside him.

"Donald, can you hear me?" she asked. "We need to talk."

He didn't reply, of course.

"If you can hear me, I need you to disconnect." Lydia knocked on his goggles.

Then she felt warmth on her upper lip. She glanced down to see a dollop of blood land on her sleeve and soak into the threads. She stood and hurried into the kitchen, grabbed a dishcloth, and wrapped ice into it. She pressed it against her nose.

Donald's voice called from the living room. "Lydia? Were you talking to me?"

She dropped the ice cube into the sink, and tucked the bloodied cloth into her pocket, and then made her way back to the other room.

Donald held his goggles in his hands, electrodes still attached to his forehead. "You're in your scrubs," said Donald. "Are you just getting home from work, or leaving?"

"It's hard to tell anymore," she said. She sat on the

ottoman beside him. "Listen. You've got to stop sending people to the clinic to ask for me."

"People need help, Lydia. The system is letting them die."

"The system is what pays my salary and gives us our health benefits. Gives us this house."

Donald's jaw tightened. "You're going to throw that in my face now?"

"No, I'm just trying to say—"

"I didn't want the housing assistance. I told you that." He set his goggles in his lap and pressed the recliner lever to flip it back up to sitting. "I didn't want this house."

"I know."

"I worked really hard at Smyth. I got in early, I stayed late."

"I remember," said Lydia.

"I took care of us. I did. And I was damn good at it."

His eyes were glassy with anger. Lydia watched him, studied the hard lines of his mouth. "I'm just asking you to stop sending people to me at the clinic," she said.

"Isn't that your job, to help sick people?"

"I got a written warning today from Dr. Rivers," said Lydia. "A *written* warning."

"You got a warning for doing what you're paid to do?"

Lydia pushed up from the ottoman. "I can't talk to you when you get like this."

"Then let me do you a favor and leave you alone." Donald slapped his goggles into place over his eyes and punched the lever to recline.

Lydia watched him for a moment, her hands clenched. Then she turned. "I'm going to bed."

"Don't wait up, little lady."

Lydia stopped, her hand on the bedroom door frame. She wasn't sure she'd heard him right.

She stepped in and closed the door.

Brian stared at the building in front of him. The siding had given up a long time ago, and the bricks and slats that were supposed to be the inside walls were the outside ones. The window frames were boarded up with plywood, and he thought that might be the only thing holding those together, too. All the shops along the street had been closed and abandoned. He would expect a street like this to be prime real estate for graffiti, but there wasn't a drop anywhere; even restless teenagers knew better than to come here.

When he squinted, he could almost read faded letters above the door that spelled "pharmacy." Must have been from when people took aspirin for headaches and shit. What did they call them? Anti-inflammatories. For backaches. Yeah.

"This is your guy?" Brian asked Donald. Donald had driven him here, made him promise not to tell anyone.

Donald reached for the door. "This is him."

Brian had a feeling that if he'd brought his Geiger, it would be clicking.

"I've been talking to him about you for a while, to help him warm up to you," said Donald. He stepped inside and held the door open, watching Brian. "You coming in?"

Brian looked past Donald into the gloom. No natural light made it through the boarded windows. There were pinpricks of lights that might have been from a control board of some kind. He thought he heard movement—a sort of *thump, drag*—but it was the smell that hammered him between the eyes. Dead things.

Brian inched back. "You know, man… I'll just wait in the car."

"Suit yourself," said Donald. He let the door close behind him.

Several minutes later, after Brian had made his way back and had been waiting nervously in the passenger seat of Donald's sedan, Donald returned. There was something different about him, like his skin was brighter, maybe. Walking a little taller in the cowboy boots he'd been bragging about for the last three days.

Donald opened the driver's door and slid onto the seat, smiling.

"You get more than a software upgrade in there?" Brian asked. "Is that the deal about this place?"

"What do you mean?" asked Donald.

"You know. Some actual Jezebels in there."

Donald blinked. "I don't follow."

Brian couldn't tell if Donald was a first-rate actor, or what, but from what he knew of the guy, he didn't think so.

Donald held up a tiny black rectangle between his fingers. "Are you ready to try tactile feedback? Sends electrical signals straight to your brain, so you can actually *feel* the gun in your hand." He smiled again.

"Where'd you get the creds for that?" Brian asked.

Donald dropped the hardware into a shirt pocket and hit the button to start his car. "I have some savings," said Donald. "Didn't I tell you I used to work for Smyth?"

Smyth Electronics, the largest U.S. conglomerate. Caught lying about trade values, sued by Brazil for clearcutting their forests, and first-rate contributor of the hydrogen cyanide milkshake this planet used to call "air." Brian never did understand why Donald was so proud of it.

"Yeah, you've mentioned a few times," said Brian.

"How about a beer with our test run?" asked Donald.

"Sounds good."

In the clinic, Lydia was sterilizing the filters in the medgrade, the large, rolling block of equipment used to administer blood and lung cleansers to multiple patients a day. They used to have three machines, but the Smyth-owned manufacturer that made replacements for the threadscreens and filtering tubes had stopped supporting Mark IV models a long time ago. So, when a medgrade stopped working, it was done for.

The one medgrade they had left had started to slow. Everyone knew it was only a matter of time before its filtering tubes started to crack. It spent more time running than it did recharging, and it hadn't been rebooted in over a week.

Paula poked her head into the back room. "Lydia, someone's asking for you at the front desk."

"Me?" she asked, trying to sound surprised. She closed the latch on the maintenance panel, wiped her hands on her scrub pants, and stood up to follow Paula.

The waiting room was full, as usual, but patients were quiet and still. Resigned, probably. Someone coughed.

At the front desk, a frail, elderly woman waited, and tried to straighten her curved spine as Lydia approached. "Are you Lydia?" she asked.

"Yes. Is there something I…"

Lydia felt a presence and knew by the pungent scent of cologne that Dr. Rivers was standing behind her. "Something we can do for you?"

The woman's eyes moved from Lydia's face to the person behind her, and back. "I was told to come ask you for a key to the restroom."

"The restroom," said Lydia, trying to hold back a sigh of relief. "We use a code at the door. Let me show you how it works." She turned. "Oh, Dr. Rivers! Would it be all right to show this patient how to use the door code for the restroom?"

Dr. Rivers narrowed his eyes, but nodded curtly, and then moved off toward his cubicle office. She watched him go until he was out of earshot, then put a hand on the woman's arm and guided her toward the restroom. "Who told you to come see me?"

The woman glanced where Dr. Rivers had disappeared as she hobbled with Lydia into the hallway. "A man named Donald. I thought maybe I shouldn't say, judging by how that doctor looked at you."

"Thank you for that," said Lydia. She stopped at the locked door. "Zero two, twenty-two," she said as she tapped the keypad. "The code is whatever the date is."

"Thank you, dear," said the woman.

"Donald shouldn't have sent you."

"Oh, I see," said the woman, peering up sideways. "May I use the restroom anyway?"

"Of course," said Lydia. "And here." She glanced around to make sure they were alone, and then slipped her hand into the pocket of her scrubs and pulled out one of her own, personal inserts. She pressed it into the woman's hand. "It's all I can do, I'm afraid," said Lydia.

"I see," the woman said again. She smiled. "Thank you, dear."

After the woman closed the door, Lydia walked to the back room to finish her sterilizing task, but when she got there, the machine had already been taken. She could hear it whirring in the treatment area. It wasn't the first time the protocols hadn't been finished before use, and she knew it wouldn't be the last.

She pulled out her stash of inserts from her pocket and counted through them. If she halved the dose for a week, she could stretch what she had left until her refill. Hopefully, her med allowance would renew at the same time, or she'd have to halve her dose again for a whole month.

The shift buzzer sounded, signaling her time to leave. She hurried to her locker to retrieve her purse, and to switch from her padded working shoes to her soft-sided flats. She made it to the biometric scanner and clocked out just in time, with half a minute to spare before she was red-flagged for working overtime.

At home, Lydia was just serving herself some leftover zucchini and rice when she heard Donald come through the front door. "Want some food?" she called. She opened a cupboard to get a second bowl.

When he didn't answer, she walked to the living room doorway to look for him. He wasn't there, but his Vee Real was lying on the couch. She walked to it and picked it up.

She turned it in her hands. The hard silicone was scuffed and dull, and it was solidly built, but hardly weighed anything. She lifted it toward the window to look through the opaque lenses, but they were as unremarkable as a pair of sunglasses.

The hallway toilet flushed, and Donald emerged from the bathroom. He stopped short. "Hey, now, don't be doing anything foolish, Mrs. Aimes."

"I'm just looking."

Donald reached out his hands and walked toward her. "Just come quietly, and there won't be any trouble."

Lydia handed them over to Donald, trying to smile at his humor. It had been a long time since they had laughed together about anything. Still, she had a difficult time seeing what was so funny. "Do you want some dinner?"

"I'm not hungry. I think I over-imbibed at the saloon."

The joke was wearing a little thin, now. "You went with Brian, right? How is he?" she asked. She returned to the kitchen to collect her dinner and sat at the table, watching him. He moved toward his recliner; his gait unsteady. He wasn't much of a drinker, so it wouldn't take much to affect him, and she hadn't ever seen him actually *drunk*, as far as she remembered. "I hope you let Brian drive you home."

He just sat in his recliner and lifted his goggles toward his face.

"Wait," said Lydia. She stood. "Let's talk."

"About what?"

"Another person came to the clinic today, asking for me." Just then, she felt wetness tickle her nose, and turned away, wiping at it. She checked her fingers. Blood. "Dammit," she said. "Just a minute."

She hid herself near the sink, out of Donald's eyeline. She wrapped another piece of ice into another dish cloth and pressed it hard to her nostril.

Then Donald was there, in the doorway. "You all right, there, little lady?"

She spun toward him, trying to read him. Did he still think he was being funny? "Actually, no, Donald."

"We don't need to have any trouble," he said.

"But there is trouble," said Lydia. "Dr. Rivers is watching my every move. He's just *looking* for a reason to let me go, and every time you send someone to the clinic to ask for me—"

"The town's full of folks needing help," he said. "A sheriff's got to do right by 'em."

Lydia moved back a step and lowered the cloth from her nose. "Are you trying to make light of this? Are you mocking me?"

Donald shook his head. "Ain't nothing light about Outlaw Bart gunning his way West. He's holed up in my town, and I got to bring him in or die trying."

"Are you out of your mind? What is wrong with you?" Lydia grabbed Donald's chin to look into his eyes. His pupils were dilated. "Oh my god." She moved her hand to his forehead. "You're burning up! Why didn't you say anything?"

"There doesn't need to be any trouble," he said. Then his knees buckled, and Lydia caught him. She pulled his arm around her shoulders, and slowly turned him around.

"Let's lie you down," she said. She helped lower him onto his recliner. "I'll get some Salisynth for your fever."

He reached for his Vee Real where it was laying on

the ottoman. "My town needs me."

Lydia grabbed at the goggles and held them out of his reach. "Don't you dare. I'll be right back." She carried his Vee Real with her to the bathroom, where she opened a packet of Salisynth. She poured him a cup of water and returned to him.

She tucked the Vee Real under her arm. "Open up, cowboy." Donald opened his mouth, where she placed the pill onto his tongue, and then offered him a drink from the cup.

She sat on the ottoman, put the Vee Real in her lap, and held his hand. "You should have said something."

"Deputy Brian," Donald muttered. "He'll know where Bart's hiding."

"Okay," said Lydia, stroking his fingers. "We'll ask him tomorrow. Right now you need to rest."

In the night, Lydia startled awake. She'd fallen asleep with her head on Donald's thigh. The distant kitchen light was still on, and also the hallway light near the bedroom. The glow into the living room was eerie, somehow, and out of place at the wrong time.

When her eyes adjusted, she realized there was a large, dried pool of blood on his slacks. She touched her face, feeling crackly and peeling, and her nose, which stung when she breathed in. Blood there, too. She'd slept in it.

Then she looked at Donald. His Vee Real was

affixed to his face. "No, Donald," she said. "Why?"

She felt his forehead. Still a fever, still damp at his hairline. She stood, stiff from sleeping hunched over, and held his chin to open his mouth and dribble some water into it. He reflexively swallowed, so she also put another Salisynth on his tongue, followed by a little more water.

Then she showered, washing the dried blood from her face and hair, and changed from her rumpled scrubs into jeans and a t-shirt. As the sky began to turn from black to gray, she dug her CommNode from her dresser drawer and pressed it to her temple. "Poplar Street Clinic," she told the house. The house, built inlaid with fiber optics and modems, called the clinic for her, and patched it through to her CommNode.

"Poplar Street Clinic," answered the clinic building.

"Message from Lydia Aimes," said Lydia. "Direct to Dr. Philip Roberts. Direct to Paula Lindstrom. Please place me on schedule hold today due to illness. Eight hours. Account number four five Charlie twelve."

"Message patched," said the clinic building. Lydia tapped her CommNode to disconnect, and after the chime sounded to confirm, she made another call.

"Brian Dennis," she said.

Brian waved at the eyeball camera at Donald and Lydia's front door. He heard the click of the door unlocking, so he nudged it open.

"Brian. I'm sorry for calling you so early on the weekend," he heard Lydia say as she approached, smiling at him.

Her smile seemed out of place on her face; her eyes looked a little swollen, she had wrinkles around her mouth, and her cheeks were sunken. He'd just been here a couple months ago, but Lydia looked like she'd aged ten years.

"It's all right," he finally said, after he'd gotten over his shock. "I'm just not sure what I can…"

They both walked into the living room, and Brian saw Donald in his recliner, his Vee Real on. Donald was sweating so much, he looked like someone had dumped a bucket of water over him. He was shivering. He moaned. He had a dried patch of blood on his pants.

"The fuck?" asked Brian. "What's happening to him? Is he bleeding?"

"That's not his," said Lydia, quietly.

"What do you mean?" said Brian. "It's yours?"

Lydia didn't respond, but she didn't have to. Brian knew. Everyone knew. First, it was nosebleeds, then, it was lungbleeds. It gets that bad, you're past help. "You haven't told him?"

"It's been a little difficult to have a conversation with him lately," Lydia said, pointing at Donald's Vee Real.

"Yeah," said Brian.

"I've been force feeding him water and Salisynth, and even gave him a click-pen dose, which hasn't helped," said Lydia. "I need to get that game off his face somehow, but I know I'm not supposed to remove it myself."

"Yeah," said Brian again, staring at Donald, feeling a slow climb of realization rise up in his neck and face. Lydia saw it, too, and her tired eyes widened.

"What, Brian? What is it?" she asked.

"That's a virus," he said.

"I'm not sure. It's not anything that's ever presented at the clinic, as far as I can tell." Lydia pressed a silicone pad to Donald's forehead, then looked at it to read digital numbers. "I want to call the Urgent Clinic, but the first thing they'll want to do is remove those goggles."

"That's a virus," Brian said again. His words were looping, because that's what his brain was doing. "A *virus*," he said again.

"Yes," said Lydia, regarding him. "Probably."

"No, a virus," said Brian. "From the bootleg." Brian put his hands on top of his head. "I knew it. God *damn* it, I *knew* it! But I let him talk me into it anyway."

"What are you saying?" asked Lydia. She walked around the recliner to stand beside him.

"He's been getting upgrades, man. The kind you should *not* be putting in your brain."

"Upgrades?" asked Lydia. "You mean for the Vee Real?" She frowned, looking between him and Donald. "I don't see how that's related."

"If you'd seen the place where he was getting his stuff, you'd know what I mean." Brian lowered his hands, pressed them to his stomach. "And I played, too!"

"You are not making any sense, Brian."

"I'm next, aren't I?" he said. He paced away, feeling his stomach hot and tight.

"I'm just a med assistant and not a doctor," said Lydia. "Or a programmer, but I'm pretty sure that's not how a computer virus works."

He turned back toward her. "Feel me." He took her hand and pressed it to his forehead. "Do I feel warm to you?"

"No," she said.

He dropped her hand. "Yeah, but you said it yourself, you're not a doctor."

She pointed again at Donald's Vee Real. "Just tell me how to safely take *off* that thing. Please. There must be an emergency disconnect, or something."

Brian felt a wave of nausea, but he closed his eyes, and breathed slowly. Then he opened them again and peered down at Donald. "It's supposed to be connected to a Vee Real server, to monitor your brain waves and shit. It makes it go on standby when there's a shift in the Gamma, Delta, and Theta." Brian now felt a headache coming on. He pressed his fingers to his temples.

"What do you mean, *supposed* to?" Lydia asked. Her voice was weak, and her face drained of color, and she was already pale to begin with.

Mixed in with his headache was a rising sense of guilt. He could have said something, done something, before things got this bad with Donald. Not just with the video game, but with how he'd been watching his friend lose his grip. "You hear about things, you know?"

said Brian. "But you don't expect it to happen to you. Or someone you know."

"What do you mean by supposed to?" Lydia asked again.

"That's the thing about bootleg upgrades," said Brian. "Undermarket stuff. You got to operate independently so the system doesn't override them."

"And that's what Donald has been doing?" Lydia sat down on a fabric-covered bench by Donald's chair.

"I did try to warn him," Brain said, hearing his own voice weak and high-pitched. Was that another symptom? Losing control of your voice?

Lydia reached over to Donald's limp hand and rested her palm on his fingers. "So, what do we do?"

"I don't know," he said. "Go in and see what's happening?"

Lydia quickly looked aside at Brian. "Go in?"

"Maybe?" Brian said. "Donald got his guy to make my VisVisor cross-play compatible. I've got Frontier Hero on my set."

Lydia stood up again. "You can go in and get him?"

Brian held up his hands. "No, man. No. I'm not going in there. Are you crazy?"

The spark of hope went out in Lydia's eyes.

"I'm sorry," said Brian, and he was. Donald was a good friend, but was a good friend worth going brain-dead for? No.

"Would he do it for you?" she asked.

Brian knew he would. He didn't say it, though.

Lydia watched Donald for a long minute. She

leaned over to kiss his forehead, then she turned to Brian. "Can you show me how it works? With your visor?"

He hesitated. He didn't want *both* the Aimes to become vegetables. But Lydia looked like she was about to start crying, and Brian couldn't deal with that. "Sure," he said. "Let me go get it from the car."

It's a dusty road in a dusty town between two dusty hills of Oklahoma territory. The sun is sharp like a rattlesnake bite, stinging your eyes, and glinting hard off the tin roof of the old watering hole townsfolk call "The Old Watering Hole."

You, [say name into device], are standing outside the watering hole, feeling the heat of the Oklahoma summer. You reach for your folding fan tucked into the bodice of your crimson dress.

You hear the clip-clop gait of a tired pony, and the rattle of a wagon coming closer. You turn to see Josiah, the farmer, pretending he can't see you, and his daughter, Jezebel, with twin braids shining like gold. She can't stop staring.

You ~~smile at her glare~~ smile at her and blow her a kiss. Jezebel gasps and averts her eyes. You ~~laugh glare~~ laugh, long ago grown used to the staring, pointing, and whispering of simple folk in this dustbowl of town called Oklahomatown. Sure, you're a saloon girl, but it's a choice you made, and most regular people don't understand. They can't see your pain, your broken heart within your sassy, hardened façade *of a* [skip]

[Player 2 Lydia join Player 1 Donald?]

[connecting]

"What will we do, Bartender Jack, if Outlaw Bart decides to ride back through?" says a voice inside The Old Watering Hole.

You push open the slatted, swinging doors of the place and step inside. Daylight shines in behind you, finding the fire in your naturally wavy, red hair. The saloon doors swing back to gently bump into your curving backside which is firm and [skip]

"I suppose we'll have to defend the town ourselves," you say sassily. Wrinkled old men, bent over their whiskeys at the bar, spin around to look at you in surprise. They only know you as the entertainment there, in the upstairs rooms, spending your nights fulfilling every [skip]

[skip]

[skip]

"Town ain't been the same since Sheriff Donald took ill," says Bartender Jack as he dries a glass with a dirty cloth. Wrinkled old men nod and murmur in agreement.

Colleen, your saloon-girl best friend, props her high-heeled foot on the bottom rung of a barstool, and pulls back the frills of her red skirt to reveal a handgun strapped to her shapely thigh. "I, for one, am ready for a fight," she says sassily.

"What happened to the sheriff?" you ask.

"Why, that mean old snake of an outlaw shot him in the back," says Jezebel.

Where did she come from? You look at Jezebel standing

beside you in the Old Watering Hole, and also in the wagon parked outside, where she sits beside her father, Josiah the farmer.

[calibrating]

"What happened to the sheriff?" you ask.

Bartender Jack and Colleen exchange a look. "We know you ain't heard yet, since you been gone to visit your sick mama in Chicago," says Colleen.

"You should talk to Jezebel," says Bartender Jack, drying a glass with a dirty cloth. "She's outside in the wagon."

You push your feminine curves through the saloon doors and step back outside into the hot Oklahoma summer day. The heat raises moisture on your forehead, dampening your fiery red hairline, and glistening between your ample breasts.

You sassily make your way to the wagon parked outside and shield your eyes from the hot sun as you turn your face up to Jezebel in the wagon seat. "What happened to the sheriff?" you ask her.

"That mean old snake of an outlaw shot him in the back," says Jezebel. "Pa and I have been caring for him back at the ranch."

"Can you take me to him?" you ask.

"It's a day's ride," says Farmer Josiah, no longer pretending to not see you. He's looking now, as though for the first time, his eyes taking in the sight of your thin waist, tightened by your crimson bodice, and the swell of your feminine hips.

"I suppose you'll be expecting something in return," you

say in that way that turns men wild with desire.

Jezebel gasps and looks away.

"Well now," says Farmer Josiah [skip]

[calibrating]

You stand in the bedroom of a 3-room shack, rough and tumble, but for the feminine touches of blowing curtains at the window, made from flour sacks, and the large, handsewn quilt on the bed. In the bed is Sheriff Donald, his eyes closed, sweat drenching his bare chest and shoulders. He's shivering.

"You saloon girls must know so much about men," says Jezebel shyly.

"What?" you ask.

"You can get them to do anything for you," says Jezebel. "With your feminine ways."

"Jezebel, could you get a glass of water?" you ask.

"Maybe you could stay here tonight," says Jezebel. "Maybe you could teach me about men."

"Oh, for Christ's sake," you say. "Jezebel, just get a glass of water."

Jezebel hurries off to fetch water from the well.

"Donald," you say, and sit beside Sheriff Donald on the bed.

His eyes flutter open. "Lydia?" he asks. "What are you…? How?"

"Deputy Brian sent me," says Lydia. "I've come to get you."

Donald coughs, spits blood. "I can't move," he says. "I've been shot in the back by Outlaw Bart. It's bad. It's real bad."

"Let me take a look," says Lydia. She takes him by his rugged shoulders and rolls him to his side to inspect his

strong back. A gaping wound, more painful than most men could endure, bleeds out onto the bed.

"No," says Lydia. "There's nothing there." She lays Sheriff Donald again onto his back. "You haven't been shot," she says.

"But it's there," says Donald. "It hurts."

"It's this ~~game~~ town," says Lydia. "It's glitching or something."

"It is glitching," says Donald. "I tried to fix it, but I failed. I'm the sheriff, I'm supposed to be the hero." He closes his eyes. "I only turned my back for a second. I thought he was down. I thought it was safe."

"Everyone makes mistakes," says Lydia.

"I promised to take care of them. I promised," says Donald, his voice a whisper. "I couldn't even do that."

Lydia's heart remembers her own ~~clinic~~ town, back home, and all the broken promises she left behind, scattered like carrion bones. She smooths Donald's hair away from his face, tanned by the rays of the Oklahoma sun.

"What's a man got left without respect?" Donald opens his eyes. They are cloudy and filled with pain. "They don't believe in me anymore."

"I think they do," says Lydia. "This town is mighty fond of you, Sheriff."

Donald is quiet for a long time, and then confesses, "You don't believe in me anymore."

"Is that...?" Lydia puts a hand to her buxom chest. "Is that really what you think, or is that a line from the ~~game~~ town?"

"What do you think?" asks Donald, looking her straight

in the eyes.

Lydia looks right back and can see it's true. Town or no town, Sheriff Donald was a ramshackle man with a bullet of shame in his heart.

"Oh, Donald," says Lydia, tears welling in her deep, dark eyes. "Whatever made you think that?"

"You've been trying to hide it. You think I don't see you're getting sick," says Donald.

Lydia puts her hand to her mouth in surprise.

"If I still had my job at Smyth, you'd have the best care money can buy," says Donald.

[Smyth information not in database]

[calibrating]

"But all you've got is your saloon job," says Donald. "Scraping by on borrowed vials. If you didn't have that, we'd have less than nothing."

But his words are empty of meaning for Lydia. She didn't cling to her saloon job just for the health benefits, she liked working for the sake of it. She sits back. "You're right, I've been sick, and getting sicker," says Lydia.

"You should have told me," says Donald.

"I guess I didn't want it to feel real," she says, clenching her hands together.

They are both quiet for a long time, while the Oklahoma wind blows dust against the windowpanes. Then Sheriff Donald sits up, and the sheet that enrobes his masculine form slides down to reveal his tight abs, and a peek at the huge, manly tool God saw fit to bless him with. He puts his rough, work-hardened hand on her shapely thigh. "I don't know how to help you," he says. "I can't fix it."

"It's not yours to fix," says Lydia. "But I need you to fight it with me. By my side." She takes his hand, and places it over her heart. His fingers rest against the curve of her shapely breast beneath her bodice. "I want you, Donald," says Lydia. "More than I've ever wanted any man."

Sheriff Donald frowns. "Is that really how you feel, or is that a line from this town?"

Lydia smiles, looking him straight in the eyes. "What do you think?"

Donald looks right back and can see it's true. Town or no town, Saloon Girl Lydia was a woman in love.

Then Donald clenches in pain and falls back to the bed.

"Donald!" says Lydia. "What's happening? Is being trapped in here making you sick, or is being sick what got you trapped?"

"I don't know," says Donald. "I tried to go home. I thought Bart was down, but then he shot me in the back."

"Try again," says Lydia.

"It's too late for me," says Donald, writhing in pain in a manly way. "Go on without me."

"Not happening, Sheriff. I came to get you, and I ain't leaving without you." Lydia leans toward him where he lies on the bed and places her hands at his temples. "Look at me," she says.

Donald looks at her, his deep, chocolatey brown eyes full of sorrow.

[server not responding]

[calibrating]

[an unknown error has occurred v1.2.0]

[Vee Reel™ and its subsidiaries are not responsible

for unauthorized modeling or coding that operates by altering base commands of Frontier Hero or any other Vee Reel™ virtual reality gaming software. To read the legally required user agreement, speak yes into the device.]

"Just say yes, Donald," says Lydia. "Maybe it will cycle you out, change your brainwaves."

"Yes," says Sheriff Donald.

[unknown error has occurred v1.2.1]

"Player 2 server connect," says Lydia.

[calibrating]

[By connecting to server, player 2 becomes host leader. Do you wish to proceed?]

"Yes!" says Lydia, clenching her fists in frustration.

[calibrating]

[waiting for server response]

[server found]

[establishing new connection]

[player 2 hardware incompatible with Vee Real™ server-based communication. Deleted code or lost memory may occur. Do you wish to proceed?]

"Wait," says Donald.

"Yes!" Lydia shouts.

[server upload in progress]

[player 2 now player 1}

{player 2 Donald connect to player 1 Lydia?]

[connecting]

[calibrating]

It's a dusty road in a dusty town between two dusty hills of Oklahoma territory. Sheriff Lydia lies in bed, her fiery red hair that matches her fiery spirit cascades across a feather pillow.

Bartender Donald sits by her side, holding a bible, quietly reading to her from Psalms. Beside him stands Jezebel, the farmer's daughter, weeping and pressing a worn, stitched handkerchief to her eyes. "I ain't never seen the Sheriff so pale," *says Jezebel.*

Sheriff Lydia bleeds from a bullet wound in her back. She opens her eyes. "It's not ~~real~~ that bad," *she says.*

[calibrating]

Sheriff Lydia has just given birth, and bleeds uncontrollably from the strain. Jezebel holds a newborn infant in her arms [skip]

Sheriff Lydia sits up, and the handmade quilt that enrobes her feminine shape falls away to reveal a peek at the generous roundness of her [skip]

"Bartender Donald? Are you with me?" *she asks.*

Bartender Donald blinks hazy eyes. He's clearly unwell, perhaps poisoned by the very swill he serves his patrons from the alcohol distillery in the cellar. "I'm here," *says Donald.*

"Player 1 Lydia and Player 2 Donald disconnect," *says Lydia.*

[confirm]

Donald felt the silicone of his Vee Real unclasp from the electrodes on his forehead. He reached up to remove it.

"Hold on," he heard a voice say. He recognized it as

Brian's voice. "Let me give you a hand. Cowboy."

"What are you doing here?" he asked. The goggles were pulled away from his face. Light hit his eyes, and he blinked, rubbed them with his fingertips.

"Lydia called me," said Brian.

"Lydia," said Donald. He tried to sit up, but he didn't have the strength, and fell back against his recliner. "Is Lydia okay?"

"I'm okay," she said from a distance. Then she came into view, looking down at him. There were red marks from virtual reality goggles around her eyes.

He reached out his hand to Lydia, and she clasped his fingers. "I'm going to get better," he said.

"Yeah," said Lydia. I've already called a MedTeam and they're on their way."

"No," said Donald. "I mean, I'm going to get better at fighting by your side."

"Oh," said Lydia.

A siren bleated outside, getting nearer.

"Do you still want me to?" he asked, squeezing her hand.

She looked him straight in the eyes. "What do you think?" she said.

A Day in the Death Of

Carl was having a hard time making himself get out of the van. Again.

He jabbed the button to kill "Dead Can Dance" off the stereo and sat with his coffee mug resting on his thigh, staring through a windshield speckled with drizzle. Beyond, detectives Hanson and Gruber hunched behind drooping police tape, squinting at each other through the morning spit, and pointing and nodding toward a body Carl couldn't see over the dashboard.

Gruber spotted him, and lifted his thick chin. Then he elbowed Hanson, who waved him over.

"A day in the life of," Carl muttered. He slid his coffee into his cup holder and grabbed at his equipment bag, and then stepped out into the wet dawn.

"What have we got?" he asked as he approached

the cops, wrestling to hold his bag and slide his arms into his Animate Response Team-emblazoned rain poncho.

"She's fresh," said Gruber. He waved away a police photographer. "No sign she's been up and at 'em already."

"Old guy found her, walking his dog," said Hanson. He scratched at his paunch. "Or, the dog did, anyway. No I.D. But she's wearing a designer label blouse, what's left of it. We think she's not far from home."

Carl peered across the copse of flowering trees that was Ingall Park, and toward the Spanish Colonial Revival homes of the affluent neighborhood. "And nobody heard anything?" he asked.

"It's not the scene," said Gruber. "She was dumped here after."

"Still," said Carl, shaking his head. He knelt to peel back the plastic sheet over the body.

It moved.

He startled, and shot to his feet. Even after all this time, it still got him.

Gruber laughed. "There she goes."

Hanson peeled back the plastic for Carl, exposing the victim's bloodied mass of hair, her flaccid mouth, her glazed eyes. Her head flopped sideways, and she jerked spasmodically.

"Gentlemen, we have us a zombie."

"Animate," corrected Carl, fumbling in his bag for his microchip scanner. "Could you guys hold her still?"

"We already scanned her," said Gruber. "I told you, no I.D."

Didn't matter, it was regulation. But he didn't explain, he just pushed at the girl's shoulders to roll her over. He only had moments before she would try to stand, and once she did that, she would be hard to manage. She was already twisting, and groans bubbled at the back of her throat.

He quickly passed the scanner down her spine but didn't get a hit until he hovered it near her right thigh. "Got her."

"Shit," said Gruber. "I swear we checked."

Designer label, designer microchip. No rich person wanted to be treated like a nameless zombie, even if they were so dead they wouldn't know the difference. "Ashley Perkins, age 21," Carl read from his scanner. "You're right. She's not far from home."

Ashley flopped to her stomach, and then scratched at the ground, trying to leverage. Her shredded and filthy blouse landed on the ground beneath her face. Her torn skirt bunched around her hips. "I hope you guys got all you need."

"We got it," said Hanson, scratching again at his paunch. "This ain't our first rodeo."

"All right, then. See you in about three hours."

Three hours to get back to the clinic, process Ashley's information, notify the family, and get her cleaned up for the family's retrieval, if they wanted her.

Some families took their animate loved ones home. Some didn't. But rich folks, they were the hardest to predict.

"Hey, George," Carl said to their resident floor sweeper, who had reached his 25th day of decomp but could still hold a broom. George—who was called George because "John Doe" wasn't interesting enough—grunted.

Carl's co-worker, Maura, entered the hallway with a metal tray. She drew up short when she spotted Carl and his sheet-wrapped guest. "Oh, hey, you used the back door?"

"Yeah, those Pro-Deathers are waving signs out front."

"They've been at it since dawn. They got nothing better to do than to harass underpaid government peons just doing their jobs? Like we've got anything to say about what happens to these corpses." Maura tipped her head toward the newcomer. "Is that the call from Ingall Park?"

"Ashley Perkins," said Carl, and he untwisted the tangle of odor-proof sheeting from her face and shoulders.

"Geez. She's just a kid."

"Her chip says she's 21, but yeah. Under all the blood, she's just a kid."

"Well," said Maura, leaning in to peer at their newest resident, "At least her boobs will be the last to go. Looks like she paid good money for them."

Carl frowned, and modestly readjusted the sheeting.

Maura lifted the tray of tubing and formaldehyde-infused saltwater bags. "I've got to finish irrigating Number 12, his left arm's down to a stump and it's not smelling any better. But if you want to stick Number 14—"

"Ashley," said Carl.

"Yeah. If you want to stick her in nine, I can clean her up when I'm done."

"Okay." He always felt weird about hosing down the fresh females. They were dead-ish, yeah, but still.

He walked Ashley toward cubicle nine, the refrigerated cell that would hold her until her family showed. She was doing really well for being just a one-hour, managing a shuffling gait and staring around herself as though she was actually paying attention. When they passed cubicle seven, four-dayer Stanley clawed at the slot in his door and howled.

Ashley darted toward him, breaking Carl's grip on her arm, and she reached through the slot to touch him. His disintegrating hands ripped at her sheet, pawed at her exposed breasts. Carl could swear they were trying to kiss through that slot. Or eat each others' faces.

"All right, all right." He put his arm between them and yanked at Ashley to separate them. "We aren't a dating service."

"I'm telling you," said Maura behind him. "Number 3 must have been some ladies' man. Not a dead woman in the joint can resist him."

"It's like they know each other or something," said Carl, squeezing his eyes shut against the smacking and clawing of two sets of sloppy, undead hands. "Little help here?"

The commotion startled George, who began banging his broom against the wall. In the next cubicle, Marge, a 10-dayer, ripped at her bloated intestines and threw the putrefied chunks at Ashley. Then Number 12, who looked a lot like James Dean, emerged from behind his unlocked door. He emitted a piercing, grief-stricken wail, and slapped his arm stump against the concrete walls in wet, red-black prints.

"Zombies don't know each other!" Maura raised her voice above the din as she pried Ashley's fingers from Stanley's door slot.

Carl threw himself against the slot, blocking it, and Ashley immediately withdrew into a glossy stare. Her head tipped forward. She drooled.

"Animates," Carl corrected, while Stanley pounded bloodied knuckles against his spine.

Those stains were never going to come out. He was going to have to start buying scrubs already pink, just to keep from spending half his lousy paycheck on clean uniforms.

"Animates. Zombies. Death-challenged," said Maura, pulling Ashley toward cubicle nine. "Whatever you call them, they still stink and whine, and got no business shuffling around past their expiration date."

"You won't last around here with that attitude," Carl called when the two disappeared behind a door.

Who was he kidding? No one lasted around here.

"Is she suffering?"

Ashley's twin sister, Andrea, sat in the clinic's visitation room on a plastic folding chair, regarding her drooling sibling. Ashley, sitting listlessly in a matching chair in the tiled room, was flanked on either side by Detectives Hanson and Gruber. Behind Andrea stood Hannah Jordan, the *Santa Leanna Times* social reporter, holding out a pocket recorder.

"We only just chipped ourselves last week," said Andrea. "It was a kind of joke." She chewed at her bottom lip, and affectionately pushed a strand of hair from Ashley's cheek.

"Had she been seeing anyone?" asked Detective Gruber. "Been having any relational issues?"

Andrea turned to the cop, her brow tight. "You think someone she knew did this?"

"Her death didn't occur at the place she was found. She was laid there, carefully, in her own neighborhood, so she would be discovered."

She looked back to Ashley, who had her willowy fingers pressed to her throat.

"God, does she remember what happened?" asked Hannah.

"I don't think so," said Carl. "Animates seem to retain some of their personality traits, something of a cell memory, but—"

"In all our investigations like this," said Gruber, "The victim never adds any help to their own murder case. She doesn't remember."

"But you can't be sure," said Andrea. "I mean, look. I think she knows me."

Ashley was patting Andrea's cheek, and giving a sort of soggy purr.

"That's the point, right?" asked Hannah, the reporter, pushing her way through the others to stand before Ashley. "You can't be sure how much of a person is retained, and how much is gone. Death isn't really death anymore, is it?"

Carl looked from face to face. "Well… the body dies. It continues to die."

"It continues to *decay*," said Hannah. "But that's no different than a wasting disease, like HIV or muscular dystrophy. And you don't put a bullet through the heads of HIV patients just to ease their transition."

Andrea gasped. "Is that what's going to happen to her?"

Carl waved both his hands. "We don't do that here. We're a care clinic—"

"That houses animates until they're shipped off to facilities that dispose of them." Hannah held her tape recorder toward Carl's face. "When they're not claimed by family, they're finished off in a government facility, isn't that right?"

"I don't have anything to do—"

"Yeah, yeah, it's not your job to know." Hannah lowered her tape recorder. "Except what if the government *doesn't* finish them off? What if they're kept as trained monkeys, used in radiation and safety experiments?"

Andrea gasped again.

"That's ridiculous!" Carl said. "They wouldn't be any kind of help. The government would need to know those sorts of affects on live people, not dead ones!"

"But Ashley isn't dead," said Andrea, tears welling in her eyes. "Look at her. She's... she's staring at me. She remembers me."

"I assure you," said Gruber, "Your sister is dead. She was battered in the head by a sharp instrument and her life left her."

Andrea openly wept.

"See here," said Detective Hanson, scowling at Gruber. "All this is a little tough to take, we know." He patted Andrea's shoulder. "Why don't we leave your sister with Carl, and we'll step into the coffee shop next door to ask you some more questions."

"She'll be all right?" Andrea asked, lifting her tear-stained face.

"Well, yes," Carl said, "But if you're going to take her home, there's an awful lot of paperwork to get started."

"Home?" Andrea looked between the detectives, and then to her sister. "I... I mean, it will take days for my parents to return from Barbados. And she'll need care, won't she? I don't think I ought to make that kind of decision by myself."

"Of course not," said the reporter, grasping Andrea's hand and offering it to Detective Hanson. "You go on with the officers here, and I'll be along to join you."

Andrea gave a forlorn look to her stupefied sister, and then followed the policemen toward the back door.

"Look," said Carl, turning to the reporter after they'd gone. "Whatever story you're digging for here, you're not going to find it. This clinic cleans them up and sends them on. That's all."

"Are you kidding?" Hannah lowered her voice. "Do you know who Ashley Perkins is? All those Pro-Deathers marching on Washington, getting celebrity funds and marathon sponsors demanding the "compassionate" killing off of—"

"You can't kill something that's already dead," said Carl.

"...and then Ashley Perkins shows up, murdered and rich and ready for the 'Animates are people too' campaign posters with her pouty lips and zombified cleavage! They couldn't have a better spokesmodel!"

Carl gently guided Ashley toward the double doors of the housing area. "I'm sure she's glad to have made your day. I have work to do."

"Come on, Carl. Don't tell me you don't sympathize." Hannah followed him, her tape recorder stuck out toward his cheek. "Why else would you still work here, after all this time?"

He paused. "It's a job. Most people need one of those."

Hannah smiled. "Most people couldn't do this kind of job." She lowered her recorder again. "You do this because you know, whatever else is going on in with those animates, they are still *people* inside."

Carl groaned, and guided Ashley through the double doors. The cold metal flaps swung back, and Hannah dodged to follow.

"I just want to hear it from you, Carl. From someone on the inside. Someone who knows they're more than just mindless freaks of nature."

Carl spun to face her, then. "But I don't know!"

At his shout, Stanley roused. He threw himself against the door of his hold, shrieking. Ashley broke from Carl's grasp, and returned Stanley's hollow cry as she darted across the hallway to thud herself against Stanley's door. They pawed and clamored at each other through the slot.

James Dean emerged from his unlocked hold, gimping into the hallway. He flailed his arm stump against the wall, and barraged a pattern of gangrenous, oily sludge.

Marge joined in, clattering her door nearly off its hinges. She scratched at her mouth, pulled teeth and rotten tongue with her bony fingers, and threw the handfuls through her iron bars.

The hail pattered against Ashley, who had pulled off her paper gown. Ashley was bent forward, howling, her backside pressed against Stanley's door, while the door bang-bang-banged from Stanley's violent attempts at dry-humping.

Carl felt a hand on his arm. He looked at Hannah, who had gone pale and quiet. Her lips parted, and she might have said something, but he couldn't be sure, with all the ear-piercing noise.

"You were saying something about people?" Carl shouted.

Hannah's brow twitched, and she pointed a finger toward his face, inhaling sharply to chastise him. But at that moment, a wedge of Marge-flesh slapped to her wrist. She froze, staring, her eyes going hazy.

Two decay-blackened nubs of fingers pinched the blob from Hannah's wrist and dropped it to the floor.

"Thanks, George," said Carl.

George grunted. Then he turned, and, with his push broom, quietly swept it away.

The color in Hannah's face evaporated.

"Here," said Carl, bracing her. "Come sit in the office while I get them under control. Then maybe we can talk more."

She nodded. "Talk more about what it's really like on the inside," she said, her voice faint. She shuffled, her gait awkward, and she leaned a little too hard to her left.

Carl led her along just fine. He was pretty good at that sort of thing.

Days later, he sat in the Animate Response Van, watching a foggy rain through the windshield. "Dead Can Dance" quietly chanted from the stereo. He sipped at his lukewarm coffee, and then rested it on his thigh. "Having a hard time getting out of the vehicle?" he asked.

Beside him, Hannah Jordan turned off the stereo,

then pushed the button on her mini recorder. "A little," she said.

"First time's the worst," he said. "But don't worry. After that, it doesn't get any easier." He smiled.

She smiled too. Then she sobered. "Are you sure you're ready to find out wherever this story leads?"

Carl wasn't, but he nodded anyway. He wondered what his job would feel like once Hannah discovered what she was looking for. He also wondered how it would feel if she didn't.

"Okay," she said. She cleared her throat. And then she spoke into her recorder. "Day one of my assignment in the ART. This is Hannah Jordan, with Carl Weedham, and *A Day in the Death Of.*"

Hologram Bride

Between 1908 and 1924, over 20,000 Asian women immigrated to Hawaii to marry Japanese sugar plantation workers. Strong restrictions in immigration laws forced workers to arrange marriages based on photographs only. The U.S. Immigration act of 1924 abruptly stopped these arrangements, but by 1930 picture bride unions birthed over 100,000 offspring—a powerful presence in what would become the 50th state of the union.

Mama Iris put her wrinkled hand over the words in my book and bent to peer into my eyes. "You're no longer a child," she said.

I pulled my book out from under her hand, spun in my chair, and pretended not to listen.

"They won't extend another year," she said. "You've

known this day was coming."

They. The Alliance Government, she meant, and they were kicking me out. Tomorrow was my 20th birthday, and I would no longer be an Alliance ward. For two years Mama Iris had manipulated a loophole to extend my wardship in the orphanage while I taught kindergarten, but those same two years I'd been repeatedly turned down for a permanent teaching post. "I don't see why they won't let me stay," I said, closing my book. "I'm a good teacher."

"You're the best teacher I've had for the little ones," said Mama Iris.

"This is the only home I've ever known, why doesn't that mean anything to them?"

Mama Iris sighed. "I don't know." She hobbled to the window and stared down into the street. Gray clouds crippled the sunlight, but it managed to squeeze through the dusty pane and deepen the furrows of her face.

She tapped her cane against the glass. Ash that had settled on the outside sill puffed into the air and sifted away. "The sickness will come to you out there, Karla. Tomorrow you will face the world without ventilated air, without breathing treatments. Without medicine."

"Are you trying to frighten me?"

Her knob of silver hair wobbled when she nodded. "I suppose I am."

"You needn't bother." I crossed my arms. "I know what you're driving at, anyway, and I won't do it. I refuse to let you peddle me away like some slave ship cargo to that horrid planet."

"That horrid planet is green and blue and full of life." She stuck the tip of her cane into a slate-colored button on the wall. My Repli-Chef. After an image shimmered into a cup of water, she popped open the door of the appliance and threw the water out onto my floor. "On Reisas, you can drink water from streams. You eat food that actually grows from the ground."

"Sounds savage." I drew up my feet into my chair.

"Savage?" Her watery eyes narrowed. I hadn't often seen Mama Iris angry, but she was angry now, and I could feel it all the way across the room. I wanted to shrink back, but instead I lifted my chin and stared right back at her.

"You come to this window and see something savage," she said.

Now I did shrink back. I avoided the window and kept my shade pulled as a rule. I didn't want to see what she was pointing at. Whatever it was.

"Now, Karla Jean."

Both names. Double whammy. I slinked off my chair and moved slowly toward her.

"Tomorrow when they boot your tiny fanny out through the gates with 100 units in your pocket, what's your plan? Eventually, when your lungs start filling with Black Death and you don't have five units left for a one-dose needle, what will you do?" She clutched the sash and yanked it open.

Ashen wind blew in, scattering papers off my desk. I coughed, feeling the air like sticky fingers down my throat. "Close the window, Mama Iris! Are you crazy?" I tried to slam it shut, but she poked my belly with her cane and pointed into the street.

"Look there, Karla. Blink the dust out of your eyes and look."

I blinked. The metal buildings across the street were stained with death pallor, the road below was a river of monochrome gray, and even the clothing and facemasks of milling people were the same bland color as the air. "I'm going blind," I whimpered. "Close the window."

"I won't let you go blind, child. I want you to see."

I coughed again, and held my hand over my mouth, breathing shallow.

"A five-piece, mister, just a five," said a husky voice in the street below.

I leaned over to find the speaker. A woman in a thin, once-red dress clung to a lamp pole. Lacy gloves covered her fingers. She caught a passing man by his sleeve. "A five piece buys your dream girl," she crooned, and smiled with a curving mouth that once might have been pretty. Now black spittle gathered at the corners, and, when the man reached into his pocket, she coughed, spewing tiny ink dots across his chest.

The man grimaced beneath his facemask. "Get off the streets." He withdrew his hand from his pocket, empty.

"Wait. How about a half five?" She followed him around the corner where they both disappeared.

I turned from the window. "Please close it."

The sash slid closed. "I sent your hologram to the

agency months ago, Karla."

I hugged my arms to myself, staring across at my slab of gray wall. "What you're doing to me is no different than what the streets would do to me."

"A Reisan has offered to bring you over. Would you like to see him?"

"No."

"He works with his hands. A carpenter."

I gritted my teeth and willed my insides to shrivel up and hide away, out of reach.

"Karla, they are a people very much like us. Like we used to be." She laid a hologram sphere on my desk.

"How can you call them people? They aren't even human."

"They're close enough."

"Close enough to breed with, you mean." I stomped to my chair and dropped into it, sending it whirling. The room spun around me, and I watched Mama Iris swim by, over and over, like a flash of pale lightning against the stormy sky of my lodging walls. "That's all the program is," I said. "They want us to think they're being kind, saving a dying people from a dying Earth, but they just need us to widen their gene pool. They buy us to breed us."

"Karla!"

"It's disgusting."

Mama Iris stuck out her cane to stop my spinning chair. "Karla Jean Tremont, where have you heard such rubbish?"

"Everyone knows it." I glared up at her. "That

Reisan freak wants me to plant his food and birth his babies like some barefoot, backwoods concubine, and you're going to let him!"

Mama Iris's eyes burned hot, and her fist clenched like she was thinking of hitting me. "You will meet me in my office at dawn with your belongings in a case that will fit into the ship's overhead compartment." She turned and hobbled toward the door.

"I hate you for this," I said.

Her hand paused on the sensor button. "I know." Then she swept her hand. My door whisked open, and she strode through.

My eyes turned to the hologram sphere on my desk. I already knew what I would see when I activated it. All Reisans had green skin, just like every bad Martian movie ever filmed. They had thick, spongy hair, unless they were bald, and immense blue eyes that were all iris and no pupil. They appeared to have arms and legs and torsos like humans, but whatever else they hid under their clothing I could only imagine. And I was going to be married to one.

I welled up out of my chair, snatched the sphere, and smashed it to bits against my wall.

Dawn came, despite my spending all night resisting it. I stood in Mama Iris's office, my eyes puffy and bleary. I didn't remember sleeping at all, but I must have, because green faces had haunted my dreams.

Mama Iris's computer display was clacking like a ticker tape, filling with lines of information about my husband-to-be. I didn't want to read it. I already planned to hate my life, and knowing what to expect wasn't going to change anything.

Finally the door creaked open. Mama Iris shuffled in followed by a green creature in an expensive-looking suit. My stomach lurched. He was even more hideous than my nightmares could manufacture. He was scrawny, with arms no thicker than a child's, and his face was lumpy with acne. His hair was marigold yellow—was that a natural color?—and it bulged out around his head like a mushroom cap.

"Oh, Mama," I groaned, clutching at her arm. "I can't do this. Don't make me do this."

Her eyes went soft and sad for a moment, and she patted my hand. "I hope one day you'll be glad for this. Not today, I know. But someday, maybe." Then she turned. "Now, Doctor Argess is here to make sure you're healthy."

"Doctor Argess?"

"Yes," the Reisan said, stepping forward to hold a silver stick toward my face. "Stick out your tongue, please."

I obeyed. "Yow nah ma hubban?" I asked, tongue flopping.

His face curled up in disgust. "Certainly not." The silver stick jolted my tongue and I startled. He looked at a blinking display on the stick. "No diseases, no genetic predispositions. Exemplary."

"I thought he'd be coming to meet me."

"And pay for two passages on the ship?" His eyebrows, or, the place where eyebrows should be, shot up, and he looked at Mama Iris. "Does she know how expensive she is?"

"She knows little of the program, but she learns quickly."

"Hm." The doctor dropped his silver stick into his suit pocket and turned on his heel. "We must hurry." He disappeared through the door.

I couldn't make my feet move. I stared at Mama Iris, waiting for her to call out and stop this, or for the sky to split and suck me up, or anything, anything at all, to keep me from doing what they wanted me to do.

Mama Iris cupped my cheek. "Be brave. When you get a chance, please satcom me. Tell me I did the right thing."

The doctor was back, tugging on my arm. I wouldn't have thought he'd be so strong, as scrawny as he was, but my feet were moving fast to keep up. Then we were outside, and Mama Iris was waving from the window. I couldn't wave back. I almost couldn't breathe. I couldn't even cry.

At the docking station, the doctor prodded me toward a metal arch. A Reisan in a yellow uniform greeted us, and the doctor held out his silver stick. The uniformed one passed a white box over it, and when it beeped, he nodded. "Ragin Dar'el. Sherament."

"Authorized," the doctor interpreted, and pointed the tip of the stick at my left earlobe. "Cross the portal into the ship. Once there, you'll sleep." A sharp jab pierced my earlobe, and I gasped, rocking back. "I'll be beside you from now until I hand you over to your husband, who will be there when you wake up."

My earlobe throbbed, and I touched it. Something metal was stuck fast. My fingertips tried to recognize it.

"It's for the scanners. Permanent." He gripped my arm again. "Time to go."

"How long will it take?" I asked, hoping he would say a lifetime.

"Six days. To you, it will feel like tomorrow."

A line from one of my favorite books came to me. Tomorrow is another day.

I awoke groggy and restless. Something soft was under my head, but my back was stiff against hard cloth. A cot. A musty-smelling cot. I pushed up to sit.

Beside me, a black girl about my age was rousing, too. She blinked at me and rubbed her eyes. "American?" she asked.

I nodded.

"I saw you on the ship. Before I passed out." She fingered the metal dot in her ear. "I wonder if we're going to the same village."

"Village?"

"Are you going to Arway?"

"I don't know."

She yawned behind her hand. "My husband is

a blacksmith. He looks strong in his hologram." She smiled. "He wrote me a letter with a poem in it. He's as nervous as I am."

"You don't look nervous."

"Neither do you. You look angry."

I turned my eyes to the room, now that my vision was clear again. The walls were white stone, with a white desk and chair near the door. I sat on a white cot, and the girl beside me was lounging on a yellow one. "No windows," I said.

"This is the recovery room. Didn't anybody explain this to you?"

I shook my head.

"It's to transition us to the atmosphere and sunlight. They gradually adjust the settings until we can breathe their air and tolerate the light levels of whatever part of the planet we're going to. I've heard they get so much sunshine in Arway they wrinkle like prunes in their old age. Isn't that something?"

"How long do we stay in here?"

She shrugged. "A few hours, I guess. I'm Shandra, by the way."

"Karla," I said. I tried to stand. My legs felt rubbery. I had to clutch the cot to keep from falling over.

"Careful. Go slow." Shandra eased her feet to the floor, too, and I noticed she had no shoes. I looked at my own feet. Bare.

"What happened to my shoes?"

"They incinerate them with the rest of your clothes, to make sure we don't bring the sickness with us."

I looked down at the baggy canvas dress I was wearing. When had they changed my clothes? I was about to ask when the wooden door of the room swung open. A chubby white man chatted with Doctor Argess and another official-looking Reisan, dressed in something like judges' robes. Behind them, several Reisan men paced in and out of view. I caught sight of a wide-shouldered one, with thick ropes of emerald dreadlocks, and strong arms. Shandra's blacksmith, no doubt. His eyes were blue, like all of the planet's creatures, but they were soft and nervous-looking. He looked as utterly lost as I felt. I couldn't help but smile, a little. He smiled back.

I leaned toward Shandra. "He seems nice. I hope you'll be happy."

"Thank you. You too." Then she gasped quietly, and I turned back to see her gazing intently at a barrel-chested one with black eyes and a wide chin. He held out a red flower. A rose, I think, though I'd never seen a real one. She giggled, accepted the flower, and took his arm.

A throat cleared behind me, and I spun to face the Reisan who'd returned my smile. He stood six inches taller than me. His sleeves were rolled to his elbows, and he wore denim pants with a rope through the belt loops. A curl of green chest hair peeked from the collar of his shirt, thick like the kind on his head. "Tremont Karla?" he asked.

I nodded dumbly. He smiled again. He had elongated incisors, like a vampire, and each tooth gleamed white behind lips a shade darker than his green face. His nose was broad, but pleasing against high cheekbones.

"I am Ragin Dar'el. I am here to marry you."

"You speak English," I said, because I couldn't think of anything else.

He nodded. "And Japanese, and I am learning Spanish. I hope to learn all major languages of your Earth."

"Why?" I hadn't even bothered to study my French lessons at the orphanage.

He blinked. Or, rather, a flash happened across his eyes that appeared to be a blink. He had no eyelids.

"Shall we go, then?" asked the white man, before the Reisan could reply.

A flash of terror must have passed over my face, because his forehead wrinkled, and he leaned toward me. "Are you ill? Your face has gone paler than a cloud."

I shook my head, because if I opened my mouth, I might throw up.

"You are afraid?"

I nodded. His voice was gentle and I hated that, because it was making me want to cry, and I was trying not to feel anything.

"You are not here by your own will, are you, Tremont Karla?"

That answer I had a voice for. "No."

His blue, pupil-less eyes searched my face, and then dipped toward the floor.

"Where's my luggage?" I asked.

"Luggage?"

"I brought a case with my things. Do you have it?"

He shook his head. "All things from your city had to be burned. The sickness is heavy there."

"Burned? Everything?" The tears I'd been fighting choked my throat. I bit my tongue, forcing them back. "It was just books! How could they carry anything dangerous?"

He tilted his head at me. "I have books."

"But those were mine. *Mine.*" Inside, I officially withered. At least I didn't feel like crying anymore.

The ceremony was two lines. It took place in another white room at the docking station. Someone in a pink robe spoke sing-songy, and the Reisan men, there were 20 of them now, repeated the odd phrase.

Funny how none of the women made any vows. I looked around at them, mostly my age. We seemed to be an American group, though one olive-skinned woman was whispering in Spanish. She was probably praying.

Shandra wiggled her fingers at me, her face bright like a new bride's should be. When her husband leaned in to kiss her mouth, she giggled and kissed him back.

"It is done," said the green one beside me. "A carriage will take us home." He led me away without trying to kiss me.

The outside door swung open to his world. Heat and light slammed so hard against my eyelids I thought my face caught fire. I hid behind the crook of my arm. "What's happening out there?" I asked, unable to pry open my eyes to look.

"The carriage is waiting for us," he said.

"Is it burning?"

"No." He touched his fingers to my back and guided me outside. "It is our day," he said. My feet stumbled up a platform.

From the platform, I ducked into a rounded box that sat atop four wide wheels, and was pulled by two horse-shaped animals a fair shade of maroon. Inside the box I could open my eyes again, though they watered. "Is it always so bright?"

"Unless it rains. You should have been acclimated in the recovery room." He frowned. "Others from your country did not need so long as you."

He was staring at me. I turned my face toward the window. "I thought all Reisans had blue eyes," I said.

"What?"

"Shandra's husband has black eyes. Others had green or yellow eyes. I think you were the only one with blue."

"Blue Reisan eyes are rare," he said. "But your eyes are blue, too."

I glanced at him. His gaze was still scouring me. "Your hair is the color of rensisals…uh, sunflowers," he said. "Your hologram didn't show it well. You looked very gray."

"I did?"

He nodded. "Your skin is like vanilla ice cream. I did not know humans could be so pale."

I frowned. I knew I wasn't a stunning beauty, but I hadn't expected to disappoint him.

"Do I look like my hologram?" he asked.

"I don't know, I never saw it." I crossed my arms, and glared out the window. "I figured you all looked pretty much the same."

"Ah," is all he said, but I could feel the pain in his voice. Any other day, I might have felt sorry for hurting him. Not today.

Our travel fell into silence. I watched the landscape, helping my eyes adjust to the brightness. As they did, I was able to see the array of colors that passed. Fields of yellow and green went on as far as I could see. The sky was a blue like I'd seen in paintings. Trees huddled in groups of green and brown, dotted with flecks of crimson buds that opened to white blossoms. I'd only seen such rich countryside in photos in old books. My own Earth had looked like this once, long before my time. Before Mama Iris's time, even. Before the rain forests fell.

At the thought of Mama Iris, my eyes filled with tears. Doctor Argess was right; it seemed like only yesterday when I saw her wave goodbye.

I felt a touch on my arm. A green hand offered me a handkerchief. I took it. I pretended my tears weren't there, and instead dabbed the cloth against my forehead, which had grown warm and sticky. "You have no fingernails," I said.

"Fingernails," he repeated, rolling the word around on his tongue. "What is this?"

"Fingernails," I said, and held out my hand toward him. "On your fingertips."

He inspected his fingers, and then leaned over to inspect mine. He reached out, curious, but I drew back my hand before he could touch it.

"What is the purpose of your fingernails?" he asked.

"I don't really know," I said.

The carriage lurched to a stop. I clutched at the seat to keep from sliding off. He swung open the door, jumped out onto the road, and lowered the platform for me to step on. I climbed down to join him.

When applause broke out, I looked up to see a crowd of smiling green faces. "Ragin Dar'el Karla!" someone announced. A musical sound, like a fife, pierced the air, and the applause turned into rhythmic clapping. Cotton-clad Reisan bodies stepped back to reveal a pathway to a small two-story hut with a shingled roof.

Bright pink flowers climbed the sides of the hut and met in a waterfall of color over the roof. An archway of woven wood stood against a slat fence. Purple and white blossoms dangled in bunches from the arch, clouding the air with an earthy-sweet scent. "This is where you live?" I asked, feeling as though I'd just stepped into one my student's fairytale stories.

"Karla!" I recognized Shandra's voice, but I had to step back onto the carriage platform and look over the heads of the crowding Reisans to find her. She was waving to me from the window of her own carriage. "I knew we'd both end up in Arway! I just knew it!"

"Come find me!" I called, but I wasn't sure she'd heard me. Her carriage was already disappearing into the horizon.

"Ragin Karla," came my husband's low voice. "We should enter now."

I made my way toward the home. As I stepped over the threshold, a chorus of shouts exploded, and I had to cover my ears. Green hands slapped my Reisan's back, and he shouted along with them in words I didn't recognize. Jolly faces peered through glass-less windows. Dried flower petals were tossed inside.

Bodies pressed so hard against the outside walls they creaked, and I was afraid they'd come crashing in. What had seemed a friendly party outside turned fierce. Feet stamped. Hands clapped. The fife screeched like a burglar alarm. My husband's arms bulged with trying to keep a stampede from swarming into the house, and I saw a leering yellow eye over his shoulder. I dove under a table.

Then I heard his voice in staccato words. A great sigh of disappointment passed through each set of lungs, and feet began shuffling away. The front door closed. The bolt slid into place.

"Wife?" he called.

I don't know why I didn't answer.

"Wife Karla?" He peered under the table. "Come out, please. It is safe."

I lowered my hands from my ears and stared into his blue, blue eyes. I didn't want to come out. Oh, but I didn't.

"You are hungry, I think. I will show you hotcakes, and then we will sleep."

"I know how to make hotcakes," I said. It was about the only thing I knew how to make without a Repli-Chef, except I called them pancakes.

"Then we will work together."

I was too frightened to eat. I crawled out anyway.

Night came, and I feared it. He stood in the doorway, watching me with that soft, nervous expression he'd had when we first met, and I'd smiled at him then, not knowing he would belong to me. Or rather, that I would belong to him. Fingering the metal clasp in my ear, I didn't smile now.

He unbuttoned his shirt as he moved toward the bed. He slipped the flannel from his shoulders and folded it neatly. His thick dreadlocks bounced against his broad shoulders, and his biceps clenched as he laid his shirt in a chair. He had a build that came from hard work, his muscles thick and strong, but not chiseled like so many statues I'd seen in books.

He sat on the edge of the bed, his back to me, and his shoulder blades shifted beneath his green skin as he removed his boots, one at a time. It was such a human sort of movement I forgot for a moment he was an alien creature from an alien world. Then he twisted to face me, and blinked lidless eyes at me, and I swallowed back an urge to scream.

He flinched as though I really did scream.

I looked away. "I came to this planet in a different solar system in six days," I said, as though he didn't already realize.

He nodded, and his head tilted a little.

"But we made pancakes on a stove we had to stoke with firewood, and we rode in a horse carriage, and you have oil lamps instead of electricity."

He nodded again. "We have technology beyond yours, but we know the arrogance of relying on it."

"You choose to live like this?"

"You were not expecting this, either. You regret your decision."

"It wasn't my decision."

"Ah. That is right." He frowned. He slid into the sheets and sat forward to rest his arms across his bent kneecaps.

"You're taking advantage of a planet that has no choice. You sought us out when it suited you, and you help us only to save yourselves."

I'd never seen an angry Reisan face, but judging by how his jaw tightened and his eyes simmered, I guessed I was seeing one now. "You presume much about my people," he said.

"A people can only be judged by its actions." I met his face like I always met Mama Iris's. Chin lifted, eyes steady.

"There is no need to anger me, Wife," he said, and flattened back against the bed, turning away from me. "I was not going to touch you."

I awoke from a dreamless sleep. A shaft of yellow stabbed through the window and glittered the hairs on my arm like gold dust. I stretched, listening to the cheerful whistles of unfamiliar birds.

Then a new sound broke through. A soft, grating sound, like wood against wood, maybe. I swung my feet over the side of the bed. I hadn't yet replaced my shoes, but the texture of the wood floor was pleasant beneath my feet, and I wiggled my toes.

I noticed a new dress over the back of the chair where my husband's flannel shirt had laid last night. My husband. Dar'el. I practiced the name in my head, formed the word with my lips. Dar'el.

There was a book on the seat of the chair with a handwritten note that read "For my wife." Seeing the word in print had more impact than hearing it, for some reason, and I picked up the note to stare at it, turn it over in my hand, read it again. I tucked the note into the cover of the book, and then leafed through the pages. I couldn't read the language, and it was broken into chunks of paragraphs with footnotes and digits throughout the text.

Next I pulled off my canvas dress, and stepped into the soft lace of my new one. Three pearl buttons clasped it shut against my throat. A satin ribbon drew it tight around my waist. It seemed too fine a dress for denim-wearing man like Dar'el, but perhaps it was a gift. A wedding gift. Like the book.

I was already in the doorway when I realized I'd thought of him as a man.

I carried the book toward the chafing sound into the backyard. I paused then, looking out over the green grass that flowed up and over a sweep of low hills in the distance. Wispy trees bent like ballerinas in the wind, reaching leafy arms in graceful arcs. I wanted to go there, to walk slowly among the trees, to feel the sun bake my skin and let the rough earth scrape beneath my feet. I was startled, because I'd never had such a thought before.

First, I had to discover the source of the gritty sound coming from the small shed behind the house. I crept toward the wooden structure and peered inside.

Through a haze of powder, I saw Dar'el bent over a slab of wood with his back to me. He was running a sheath of knobby paper over the wood, smoothing it in long, rhythmic strokes. He'd stripped his shirt, and pine dust clung to the sheen of wetness across his skin. For a moment, my breath caught. Then I remembered myself. I refused to be attracted to him. He was green and horrid.

"Dar'el?"

He cast a look at me over his shoulder. Then he straightened and faced me fully. Wood chips clung to his cheeks and to his green chest hair gone curly with perspiration. His eyes were wide and startled as they took me in.

"It's a lovely dress," I said, though I suddenly had the urge to cover myself with my arms.

He turned his eyes back to the slab of wood. "I was not sure it would fit," he said.

"It does."

He nodded, still looking away.

"And you've given me a book. I can't read it. What's it called?"

"It's a book of my faith."

"Oh." After an awkward pause, I smoothed my hands over my hips. "This dress seems awfully nice to be working in."

"Working?"

I crossed toward him, crunching wood shavings with my feet. "Won't I be keeping house, or helping in some way? Maybe I could learn to smooth wood, like you're doing."

"You would use your hands to learn a trade?"

"Of course. Don't the other women around here do that kind of thing?"

Dar'el drew the heel of his hand over his brow. "There are only three females in this village, and two of them arrived yesterday."

I frowned, trying to comprehend.

"You know the state of our people," he said.

I actually didn't. "What's happening to you?"

"For years our elders have been dying, with no babies to replace them. We have tried to undo the damage we have caused ourselves, but we can not mend all things without help."

"What kind of damage?"

"Advancements that have eaten away at Reisas, much like how your Earth suffers, and chemicals that have eaten away at Reisans themselves."

"So," I said, curious despite myself, "...how are you trying to mend?"

"Many believe our low-technology course of action has helped reverse the state of the planet. Some governments have forced their citizens to live without electricity and common convenience, but it has not come to that in Flayete Region. There will always be those who can not bring themselves to leave the cities, but more citizens choose to settle into free land each year."

"Like you," I said.

He nodded, turning back to his sanding.

"So you're a pioneer." I smiled.

He paused with his hand on the timber. "As are you," he said, and the tips of his white incisors peeked out when he returned my smile.

A knock sounded on the door, and then a face poked in, surrounded by chunks of dark, springy hair that drooped into yellow eyes. Familiar yellow eyes. "Ragin Dar'el? Vech tet rushtamen."

"Tet turashtanet, Alen Ra'nen." He laughed, and gestured the Reisan in. "Karla, my friend Ra'nen."

"A pleasure," I said to the creature that resembled a green sumo wrestler. I was surprised the man could squeeze through the doorway.

"Pleasssure," the man echoed, his yellow gaze scorching down my dress. The skin at the back of my neck puckered. I scooted closer to Dar'el.

"Juresh tayet te reminot es?" Dar'el asked.

Ra'nen shook his head, but stuck out his fat hand for a shake. "Winish. Ken katet sho ranna mishaket es winish en vet. Soo venna tet fah."

Dar'el gripped his friend's hand around the wrist. "Ah, des. Des ret."

Ra'nen beamed brightly, then hiked up his trousers around his bulging belly and nodded. "Des ret, tet." He leered at me. "Pleasssure," he said. I'm sure I saw him suck a blob of spittle out of the corner of his mouth.

I looked at Dar'el, but he didn't seem to see it.

The fat Reisan squeezed back outside.

"He has invited the village to a dinner in our honor, and Van'el's and Shandra's. Tonight, in his barn."

"That's nice of him," I said, though I had a creepy feeling. "Are you going to be working long out here? I was thinking of walking in the hills across the field."

"How long would you like me work?"

I smiled. "No, I meant, maybe you could go with me."

"You wish me to join you?"

"That's what I said, isn't it? Is my English so bad?"

"For a moment, I doubted my own." Dar'el returned to sanding his plank of wood. "I will need half the morning to finish the bed frame for Dresh K'tarn."

"In the meantime, I'll learn my way around the kitchen, and the mystery of heating water for your bath when you're finished."

He paused and regarded me.

"It's the least I can do. You've been very kind."

"Do you mean it is the least you can do, or the most you can do for me?"

I couldn't hold his gaze. I turned for the door. "You regret your decision, too, don't you?"

"It was not my decision, either."

I was afraid to ask him to explain. He returned to his sanding, more vigorous than before, so he wasn't going to take the initiative. Just as well. I don't think either of us wanted to talk about it.

Reisas was blessed with two moons that turned layered shades of pink and gold as night fell. The landscape sucked in the moonlight like a desert drinks rain, and the whole area took on an ethereal glow. Dar'el's skin effused with the radiance, turning a pale beige color that looked almost human. As long as I didn't look him in the eyes, I could almost pretend he was.

He walked me across a field of yellow grass that tickled my knees. "If I didn't know any better, I might think you're keeping me barefoot on purpose," I said.

He glanced at my feet. "I didn't put your shoes out with your dress?"

"I didn't see any."

He walked quietly for a time, and then he laughed. Or, rather, he squeezed his lips together, trying not to laugh, but it snuck out. "I thought it was a custom of Earthlings to go without."

I smiled, too. "I thought it was some weird initiation ritual."

He shook his head, his smile lingering. His eyes had turned gold beneath the Reisan moon, and I saw them roving my face, searching.

Then his face turned away, and he looked ahead at the path. "There is the barn. Sounds like they started the party without us."

He was right. The ground was vibrating from staccato drums. When he opened the door, twittering melodies of what sounded like flutes and clarinets were so intense, I wondered if the village had hearing problems.

"Oh, Karla!" Shandra's voice managed to squeal over the thunderous music, and I peered at the crowd, trying to find her.

"Don't you love this village?" Her hand found my shoulder and spun me around. Her smile glowed like Dar'el's skin beneath the moon, and her brown eyes were wide, happy.

Seeing her face, I wished I did love it. I wanted to be able to smile like that.

"You're still angry," she said, her glow fading.

"I'm glad you're happy." I touched her hand. I didn't want to spoil things for her with my gloominess. "Are you going to dance?"

"Yes, I think so. Van'el went to find me a drink."

I regarded her bright face while her eyes combed through the milling bodies for a glimpse of her husband. Her expression struck a realization. "Shandra... do you love him?"

She turned, her dark brows arched. "Is that surprising? I am married to him."

"But you only met him yesterday!"

She smiled. She lifted a thin shoulder in a helpless shrug. "He's so gentle."

I stared, unable to process the thought.

"Did you know the only other woman in this village is such an old crone she hardly comes out of her shack?" Shandra leaned in to whisper. "We're the first young females some of them have ever seen. Can you imagine?"

I shook my head.

She smiled again. "I thought it would make Van'el hurried and clumsy. But he wasn't." She sighed, and touched her brown fingers to a hint of blush on her cheeks.

"Ugh! I don't want to know!"

Shandra laughed. "Come on, don't tell me you and Dar'el haven't…" Her voice trailed, and she blinked. "No! Didn't he…?"

I crossed my arms. "I didn't want to and he knew it. I don't want to talk about it."

She shook her head. "Amazing."

"Amazing for not sleeping with someone I don't know?"

Shandra saw Van'el coming and took a step to meet him. She tossed a look at me over her shoulder. "I didn't mean you."

I was just about to say something witty when I felt a yank on my arm so hard I thought it would pull out of the socket. I was dragged through the barn door, too busy fighting to keep on my feet that I couldn't get a good look at who was man-handling me. Until moonlight washed over the features of the chubby arm that gripped me. "Let me go," I said, recognizing the leer of Dar'el's sumo wrestling friend.

He pulled me toward a shadowed cleft between two field boulders. He wedged me in while I kicked at his chest and clawed at his face. Now I knew what fingernails were for. "Let me go!"

"Durashtatat," he growled, and gripped immense fingers into my hair. "Pleasssure."

I screamed and writhed. I was not going to let this fat freak have any part of me. I did not come millions of miles to a new home just to be ripped to shreds like could've happened on Earth where I would have preferred it! I lunged at his face and bit hard onto whatever green flesh was closest to my mouth. I felt something soft. I clenched.

He howled. He yanked back, dragging me with him. He flopped to his back, and I landed onto his soft belly. But I was still attached, and the best I could figure, I was latched onto one of his many green chins.

"Karla!" I head Dar'el's voice and the soft thud of his hurrying feet. His hands pried me loose and drew me back, wrapping his arms around my middle. "Ra'nen! Ils a tet duran enem!"

"Let me at him!" I twisted in Dar'el's grip, trying to claw out Ra'nen's eyes. But Dar'el walked backward so I couldn't reach. Ra'nen climbed to his feet, his chest heaving. Dark blood dribbled from his chin.

He stuck a plump finger at me. "Human girl is my turn!"

Dar'el set me down, but guarded me behind him as he inched forward to hiss at his friend. "Sssshayan, Ran'en." He threatened a fist at the fat one's face, his nostrils flaring. "Ssssshayan."

More thundering footsteps gathered, and soon all those from the barn were crowding around, pointing or gaping. Shandra wedged through them to grip my shoulders and pull me back. "Karla, what happened? Are you okay?"

"I'm fine." But I was trembling so hard I could hear my bones rattle inside me.

Dar'el swept a glare over the gathered Reisans. "Shayan! El yuritet!"

Now Van'el emerged from the wall of men, and moonlight bathed his face, his features pained as he looked from Shandra to me. "An. Anyetel arn reshtitet," he said.

"He says we have a right to know," said Shandra.

"Know what?" I stared at the faces around me, trying to figure out what was going on.

"I don't know." But her voice sounded as though she had a pretty good guess. She released my shoulders and hurried toward Van'el to wrap her arms around his chest. He hugged her and disappeared with her into the crowd.

"Know *what*, Dar'el?" I reached a shaking hand toward his arm.

He glared once more at his friend, and then guided me quickly across the field and toward the house. "I am sorry. It still does not give him the right to act like a…"

He snarled, his face twisting while he searched for the word. "Mongrel," he finally said.

My feet stumbled to keep up. "You're scaring me."

He slowed. He stopped altogether. The crowd stayed back, a shadowed lump in the far distance. After glancing backward, he cupped his hand over my shoulder. His palm was rough through the fabric of my pretty dress. "Let us get inside. I will pour you a cup of seed wine."

My stomach turned to rock. Suddenly I had a pretty good guess, too. We went inside.

In the kitchen, seated in a wood-woven chair at the table Dar'el's own hands had built, I cupped my hands around my mug of seed wine and stared hard into his weary face. "You're telling me I'm supposed to be *shared?*"

He flattened his wide hands against the table, and sucked in a breath to speak. But he only shook his head, lifted his own mug of wine, and drained it dry. He drew his fist across his mouth. "Not one of us could afford a wife's passage for ourselves. When we pooled our money, we had enough for two."

"Two for a village of twenty men?" I stood, pressing my fists onto the table, clenching my fingers so hard it hurt. "Passed around like dinner plates? Taking *turns?*"

He reached for the jug of wine and refilled his cup. His hands were shaking.

"A five-piece buys your dream girl," I snapped.

He looked up. His brow wrinkled, and his blue eyes flashed with a lidless blink.

I laughed, but I didn't think any of this was funny. "Mama Iris thought sending me here would keep me from selling myself for medicine." Instead, I was to be passed around for free. I was so angry I didn't even have words for it. But I had a mug. I hurled it with all my strength at the closest wall. It didn't shatter, but it splashed wine and landed with a satisfying thud.

Dar'el startled. He came around the table, his green hands outreaching. I saw him close in, and just then I did want him to hold me. I wanted him to say he understood and he would fix everything. But instead I felt my upper lip curl. I recoiled. "Don't touch me."

He didn't. He lowered his hands. "Karla—"

"I won't do it. I don't know if the program people think they can force me somehow, but there's no way I'm going to do it."

"The administrators were supposed to have explained this. You were supposed to be a volunteer."

I gaped. "Are you kidding? Who would volunteer for that? What kind of animals do you think we are?"

"Not animals—"

"And what about poor Shandra?" I wilted a little, thinking of her. I had to sit again, because my legs went soft. "She loves him. She won't want to be with anyone else, either."

The chair across from me creaked as Dar'el sat again, too. "She loves Van'el? Is this true?" he asked.

"Yes. I don't suppose that means anything to you."

His jaw tightened. "Of course it does."

"But not to Arway. You didn't bring us here to love us; you brought us here to use us." I stood again. "You're more human than I gave you credit for."

He opened his mouth, but I left before he had a chance to speak. Whatever he had to say wouldn't make me feel any better, anyway, and couldn't make me feel much worse. I paused outside the bedroom door with my fingers on the handle. "In the morning, you'll take me to the processing station place and get your money back."

He stood. He turned to face me, his hand resting on the back of the wooden chair. "I do not think they will—"

"They'll have to do something, because they gave you the wrong girl." I opened the door and closed it hard behind myself. I stood, shaking.

I heard his footfalls through the door. He came close, and I whirled to watch the handle. He wouldn't follow me in, would he? My eyes searched the room for something weapon-like, but he only knocked quietly.

"Karla?"

I crossed my arms and silently dared him to come in.

"Would you mind me getting my pillow and my reshka? I will not stay."

His voice was soft and hesitant. Somehow, it cooled my burning anger. I considered. Then I clicked open the door. I glared at him so he'd know he wasn't in any way forgiven.

My expression was wasted, because he didn't even look at me. He went straight to the bed and pulled off his pillow, and then he knelt and searched the floor. He reached beneath the bed.

"What's a reshka?" I asked. Maybe if I helped him find it, he'd leave sooner.

"My book of faith. Like the one I gave you."

"Like a bible?" I remembered, though I hadn't read any of it. I didn't know the language, but I'm not sure I'd have read it if I did.

"Yes, bible." He held up the thick book he'd found beneath the bed. He stood and turned for the door.

"It talks about what... your god? In there?"

He nodded, and paused in the doorway. "The God of creation who made your world and mine."

"Really." I didn't think anyone believed in a Supreme Being kind of thing anymore—but then Reisas was a strangely mixed planet of technology and simplicity. I supposed if any kind of mystic faith survived somewhere, this was as good a place as any. "So you believe in a big plan of some kind?"

He nodded again. "Yes."

"And your god, how would he feel about your village sharing me around? Would he approve?"

Dar'el stared hard at the floor with his pillow in one hand and his reshka in the other. Then he lifted his gaze to look directly at me. "No. No, he would not."

I had more I wanted to say, but he slipped backward through the doorway and turned into the small room off to the right. A living room of sorts, with a fireplace that wasn't lit, and a long couch of wood and soft cushions. I'd explored that room earlier, searching for the store of books he'd alluded to when we'd first met.

Was that only yesterday? Our first meeting? I was weary as though I'd spent countless lonely days on this foreign planet. I wanted to sleep, but not in the nice dress Dar'el had given me. I also didn't want to wear the scratchy canvas shift I'd been given. I would have to raid Dar'el's wardrobe.

The tall wooden structure loomed against the wall near a floor-length window. As I came closer, I noticed intricate designs along the front panel, carved in relief to appear as a shower of tiny leaves. I had to touch the leaves because they looked so real.

I opened the panel to find an array of cotton shirts on hangers. All shirts were the same, collared version in three colors. I chose a blue one. The fabric was soft flannel, and the small buttons fastened smoothly.

When I closed the wardrobe, the falling leaves on the door again caught my eye. Such attention to detail. This was no piece of ordinary furniture, it was created to be beautiful. The realization made me examine the bed. I had to bring a lantern closer to see the headboard in the darkness, but I did find the same leafy pattern. Again I had to run my fingertip over the wood to remind myself they weren't real.

What other leaves were strewn through the house? My curiosity won out over my weariness. I carried the lantern into the short hallway that led to the kitchen.

Sure enough, the same falling leaves cascaded down the backs of the kitchen chairs. More tiny leaves decorated the four corners of the kitchen table.

I wandered a little, searching for the pattern like a hidden treasure, and each time I found it, I smiled. On a small shelf by the front door. In the handles of the kitchen cabinets. I was working my way back down the hall when I noticed a glow coming from the living room. I paused.

Dar'el was on his back on the couch, one arm dangling downward. A quilt covered his legs and draped to the floor. There was no fire in the hearth. The glow that had caught my attention was the wash of pure moonlight through a large window, golden-pink, and so bright I almost didn't notice Dar'el's lantern still burning on the floor beside him. I set down my light and moved into the room.

He made a low sleeping sound. His reshka was open against his bare chest. His eyes looked open, staring right at me, and I paused, startled. But there was a dull film over his eyes, and when I wiggled my fingers, he didn't respond. So I knelt, lifted the glass cage of his lantern, and blew out the flame.

I looked closer then, as I knelt. I wanted to be angry with him still, but one dreadlock dangled down the bridge of his nose, and one arm rested beneath his head, showcasing the bulge of a strong bicep.

I stayed, watching him sleep, bathed in moonlight. Then I reached for his reshka. His limp fingers rested on the book's spine, and I had to ease that hand aside, laying it onto his belly, instead. I carefully lifted the book and closed it, and set it silently onto the floor.

He shifted. I looked back to his face. His brow wrinkled faintly, and then the filmy coating over his eyes split open and slid out of sight. He was awake. He tensed, watching me as though I might slash him through the heart.

I rested my hands on the edge of the couch to show him I wasn't holding anything sharp. "I was just moving your book. You fell asleep reading it."

He continued to watch me.

"And you left your lantern burning. I blew it out."

He narrowed his eyes.

"Are you cold?" I grasped his quilt to pull it over his chest, but he laid his hand over mine and stopped me.

"What are you doing here?" he asked.

"I was in the hall, and I saw your lantern and then your book. I told you."

His grip on my fingers loosened. "You could not sleep?"

I could have, if my treasure hunt hadn't distracted me. "Did you make the wardrobe in the bedroom?"

He brushed the wayward dreadlock away from his nose. "The wardrobe in the bedroom? Yes."

"And the bed, and the kitchen chairs?"

"Yes. What time is it? Is it early or late?" He drew his arm from beneath his head and worked the stiffness out of it, then sat up. The quilt fell down around his hips. The top of his trousers peeked out.

"Late. You've only been sleeping a few minutes, I

think. Dar'el...?"

He arched his spine to stretch, and kneaded his fingers against the back of his neck. "Hm?"

"How long ago did you make your furniture?"

He swung his feet to the floor, looking around himself as though trying to orient. The quilt stretched across his lap, and he jostled to loosen it. "Around the time I built the house. The wardrobe was the first and the rest came in projects after."

I smiled. "They're very beautiful. I found the leaves in the kitchen, too, and I had to touch every one because they look so real."

"You like the leaves?"

"Yes. In the orphanage everything was cold metal, and we didn't waste units on much decoration. Wood furniture is so rare I didn't really understand the difference until tonight."

"What difference?"

"The difference of things created by human hands." I reached for his fingers. "Or, Reisan hands. Or whatever." I turned his palm upward, and he let me. I traced my finger pad over the thick creases and calluses of his skin.

"Karla."

I lifted my gaze to find his eyes. They were wide and frightened. "What's wrong?" I asked.

"What are you doing?"

I didn't really know. I released his hand and stood. "I'm sorry. I wasn't thinking, I guess."

He tried to rise, wrestling with the quilt to free

himself. "You are not yourself."

"What do you mean?"

"To not think. It is not like you."

I watched him carefully fold the quilt, and felt each casual move of his arms as a stab in my chest. I'd wanted him to *want* me to touch him. It had never dawned on me he wasn't interested. "I'm sorry," I said again, and walked toward the hall.

"You are wearing my shirt," he said behind me.

I scooped up my lantern and peered over my shoulder. "I didn't want to sleep in my dress. Is that okay?"

He smiled. "Yes. You look better in it than I do."

I smiled a little, too, but I couldn't tell if he was just trying to make me feel better.

He took a step toward me. "Karla, I do not want you to leave."

"No, you're right. I wasn't thinking, and it's not like me. I shouldn't have woken you up."

He shook his head. "No, I am trying to say—"

Pounding erupted on the front door. "Ragin Dar'el! Farin et! Su en Baren Van'el!"

I startled, but Dar'el outright jumped. "It is Van'el." He brushed past me to move quickly to the door. He slid the bolt. "Jurnesh es nayata?" he asked, creaking open the door.

Van'el began speaking before the door was fully open. His color was pale, his black eyes wild with panic. Dark blood oozed from a cut in his forehead, and his shirt was torn away from another wound near his ribs.

"Vaynar du eshua min eldradet! Kin laren…say rayin shurinel…"

"Shandra?" asked Dar'el.

"Ay. Resta may."

"What about Shandra? What happened?" I hurried toward Dar'el and clutched his arm. "Is she all right?"

"I have to help Van'el. You stay here." Dar'el tried to pry my fingers from his arm. "Stay here out of sight."

"Why?"

"No," said Van'el, and pointed at me. "They come next for her. Listen."

Angry shouts sounded in the distance. They were gathering, and getting closer. "What do I do, Dar'el?" I squeezed even harder on his arm.

"I will go with Van'el and make them think I have you. When they follow me, you go out the bedroom window and run into the trees. Go straight without veering until you find a small hut with a painted roof. There lives our Nanayant. She will protect you."

"What about you? What about Shandra?"

"We will find Shandra, and bring her to the Nanayant. Which is what we should have done in the beginning." Dar'el cast a dark look to Van'el, who lowered his head. Dar'el reached for a hoe handle resting beside the door, and looked back to me again. "You are strong, Karla. No matter what you hear, run for the trees and do not stop. Understand?"

"Yes."

"Go now and listen for the men to turn."

I hesitated, watching his face and suddenly wishing

I'd let him kiss me a long time ago.

"Go, Karla."

I turned, lantern in hand, and ran for the bedroom. The front door clicked shut.

The bedroom window was already ajar. I pushed up the sash as quietly as I could. I stood listening, hearing angry shouts and the overwhelming rush of the oncoming men. Just when I thought they must be at the door, another yell broke out, joined by an echo of unfamiliar words. Pounding feet moved off, and the voices grew distant. They'd turned, just as Dar'el said they would.

I crawled through the bottom half of the window. I was mildly aware that my knee scraped something sharp, but I was on my feet and running for the trees without hesitating. I watched the forest shadows bounce closer and closer, trying to judge the distance. Several yards. Lots of running strides in bare feet.

I hadn't had a reason to run before, and by the time I hit the treeline, my lungs burned and my ribs ached. I paused to catch my breath and to listen for the sounds of the men. Moonlight helped me make out the shape of Dar'el's house when I turned to search. I saw the black rectangle of the shed. A dark shape moved between the buildings. Then a lantern light swung toward me and lit my ankles. A voice called out.

I'd been spotted. I found the strength to run again, despite my struggling lungs. Dar'el had told me to run straight without veering, and I did. I hopped over fallen logs and climbed up and over craggy trunks, searching in the darkness for a way I didn't know and a hut I'd never seen before.

A glimmer of something caught my eye, then blinked out. I paused, panting, trying to decide if I'd imagined it. Then a breath of wind rustled low tree branches and through waving leaves I saw it again. Torchlight. In a rectangle shape, like a window. The hut!

I didn't hear anyone following me, but I didn't trust the silence. I lunged for the hut. I stumbled over something and landed on my hands and knees, right at the doorstep. The door swung open. A face like a pale honeydew melon peered down at me.

"You must be the bride," said the crone.

I got a strange feeling she was surprised, or maybe disappointed, to see me.

"Come, I'll make tea." She drew me to my feet, though she didn't look like she ought to be so strong.

She shuffled inside. Her dress was a robe, and it hung off her frame and puddled around her feet, looking made for someone twice her size. Maybe over time she'd shrunk inside it and hadn't noticed. Her spine was arched, her hands withered. Her frizzy hair was the color of butter. "You bleed," she said.

I looked down at my kneecap. A shallow gash oozed crimson down my shin. "It doesn't hurt."

"It will. Sit." She pointed to a chair, and I obeyed. She scuffled into a brightly lit corner and pulled a gingham blanket over a sculpture of twisted pipes. Then she opened a small trunk on a table.

I looked around the room. That's all it was, really; a

single room with a cold fireplace, a bed, a small kitchen-like counter with cupboards and tools on the wall, and a table. It was no bigger than Dar'el's shed.

"I think the men have hurt Shandra," I said. "Can you help her?"

"How?" The woman looked over her shoulder at me while her hands busily gathered small tins.

"I don't know. Should we look for her?"

Knocking exploded on the door. The woman pointed a gnarled finger. "There she is now."

I bolted out of my chair and yanked open the door. Sure enough, there was Shandra. Blood on her cheek mixed with wet tears. "Shandra!" I hugged her. I couldn't help myself.

She whimpered and pulled back. I saw then that her shoulder was bleeding, too. "What did they do to you? How did you get away?" I urged her toward the chair I'd just vacated.

"I'm okay. I don't think they meant to hurt me, they were just so angry," said Shandra, sitting hard into the chair.

"Not angry," said the old woman. She hobbled toward a rain barrel sink and pumped water into a wooden mug.

"I couldn't understand what they were shouting. They were dragging me."

"If not angry, then what?" I asked, watching the woman carry the mug to Shandra. Shandra took it with shaking fingers, but just stared off toward the wall.

"Then they released you?" asked the woman.

"I heard Dar'el's voice. And Van'el. Then more shouting and tugging on me, and then no one was watching me. I found a lantern somehow. Funny…I don't remember picking one up."

"Why would they hurt her if they're not angry?" I asked.

"I realized I was near Karla's house, so I crept around back. I saw her go into the trees."

The woman frowned. "They didn't follow you?"

"Hey," I said, and rapped on the woman's arm with my knuckles.

"I am Nanayant Elt Dor'is. Not 'Hey'." She sniffed, and scuffled back toward her collection of tins.

"Ohhh, you're the Nanayant," said Shandra. "I should have guessed. But, why haven't we met you until now?"

"I don't like visitors." Dor'is smeared brown speckles into a white ointment, and then crooked a green, wrinkled finger at Shandra. Shandra stood slowly, set down her mug, and obeyed. "That scratch will scar. Your skin is so dark." She smeared the ointment over Shandra's cheek.

"Van'el likes my skin."

"Let me see your shoulder."

Shandra unlaced the ties of her cotton blouse and tugged the fabric down her arm to expose a jagged tear. She winced a little when Dor'is shoved more ointment into the wound, rough and quick. Then she pulled her blouse into place. "You should have been the first to bless us."

Dor'is waved away Shandra's words, then hobbled toward me and offered me the tin. After I took it, she continued past me toward the cupboards. "All the men of Arway bought you, all the men should share you."

I jumped to my feet. "You know about that?"

"Of course she does," said Shandra. "The Nanayant knows all decisions concerning her village."

"Bah. Don't make it sound so noble." Dor'is slid over calico fabric from a low cupboard to expose a Model III Repli-Chef. "You girls want Earl Gray or Darjeeling?"

Shandra and I exchanged looks.

"Darjeeling it is." Dor'is tapped the screen. Seconds later she opened the door of the white appliance and drew out a tray with three teacups. She scuffled over to set the tray on the table, took her cup, and blew across the hot surface. "I used to oversee the production of those, you know. For Alliance suppliers. And not just Repli-Chefs, but Steama-spanders and Inverseaffects, too. I've worked at a lot of interesting places."

"You haven't lived here all your life?" Shandra asked.

Dor'is tugged me out of the way of the chair. "Let an old woman sit, eh?" She lowered into the seat with a groan. "I've been here about six years now."

"But a Nanayant is supposed to be a matriarch born and raised in the village." Shandra said.

"So you read the brochure." Dor'is snorted. "Bureaucratic drivel. There haven't been matriarchs this side of the Walen'al River in generations."

"Who was the Nanayant before you?"

Dor'is sipped at her tea. "Wasn't one, far as I know. Old women die off out here in the wilderness all the time."

Looking at Dor'is's wrinkled face, I wondered how much older "old" was supposed to be.

"So why are you here?" asked Shandra, who had wandered her way toward the hearth and was crouching down to sit.

Dor'is set down her teacup. "Not that it's any of your business, but I was sacked."

I blinked. I looked at Shandra.

"Fired. Let go," Dor'is said. "And then banished to the outlands like some kind of criminal and left to die off."

"Then how did you make it to Arway?" Shandra asked.

"She *means* Arway," I said.

Dor'is stared at Shandra.

"She likes it here," I explained.

Then Dor'is stared at me. I shrugged.

"I'd have starved already if I hadn't smuggled my own Repli-Chef in a flour bag stuffed inside a fruit barrel," said Dor'is.

"Do the men know about that?"

Dor'is shook her head. "They know what they're told. They're almost as easy to manage as a factory of appliance robots. At least, they *were*."

"But you're the Nanayant. You can make them stop fighting." Shandra said.

"I stopped dealing with males' affdesfals a long time ago. I'm not going to start now."

I looked at Shandra. "The what?"

Shandra shrugged, and looked toward Dor'is.

"That isn't in the brochure," said the Nanayant. "Wouldn't do for Earthlings to find out how dangerous the exchange program can be for your women, now would it?"

"Dangerous?" I asked, and looked at Shandra. She was watching Dor'is.

"Might put a damper on the plan. Or cease it altogether." She set down her empty teacup and retrieved one that had been meant for Shandra or me. I didn't want it, anyway. She rose out of the chair with a grunt and shuffled toward a window. "What you witnessed tonight wasn't anger, exactly."

"You said that before."

"It's more of a frenzy. A response to the influx of hormones induced by mating season."

I grimaced.

Shandra rolled her eyes. "Like testosterone. Earth males have the same thing."

Dor'is shook her head. "Like testosterone, but not the same thing. There's a powerful chemical that stimulates their insular cortex. Makes them aggressive. Possessive."

"Destructive?" I asked.

"That's a lot of 'ive's," said Shandra.

"Let a chemical like that eat at a male's brain long enough, makes them flare. That's affdesfals."

"That friend of Dar'el's attacked Karla tonight, before the whole group of them came after me," said Shandra.

Dor'is turned from the window to regard me. She gestured toward the hem of Dar'el's shirt against my thigh. "Were you wearing that?"

"No!" I tugged at the shirt, trying to cover more skin.

She turned back to the window. "The males respond to females coming into season—we call it ripening—when breasts develop and hips widen." She sipped at her tea. "She mates if she chooses. After some weeks, female hormones decrease, the season passes, and breasts and hips diminish again."

"Diminish?" I asked.

"Females return to who they are supposed to be. Until the next cycle."

"How long is it between cycles?" asked Shandra.

"What do you mean by 'supposed to be'?" I asked.

Dor'is watched the night sky through the window. "The cycles are months apart. Years, sometimes, if you're lucky." She paused, her face collecting shadows. "I wasn't so lucky."

"Lucky?" Shandra asked.

"What do you mean by 'supposed to be'?" I asked again.

Her eyes darkened. "Ripening confuses things. Makes a female lose sight of important things, the real things." She shook her head, glaring at the stars. "I'd worked so hard for so long, earning my way into an overseer's position at the capital. I knew what I wanted. I could think on my feet. React. Stay level-headed." She turned those darkened eyes over her shoulder toward me. "I was important, you know. Like so many other females. Smart. Analytical. I was using the brain I was meant to have."

I didn't respond. I was trying to figure out which brain she was using now.

"But hormones come whether you want them or not, don't they? Turning strong females into gibbering flirts. Turning gentle males into mindless beasts," she said. "You try denying the feelings your body is convinced you have!" She stabbed an accusing finger toward my face. "Feels like love. Feels like sacrificing everything you've ever wanted is the right thing. But it's just chemicals," she said, and then she rapped her index finger against her temple. "Chemicals."

At that, her glare faded, and she looked between Shandra and me. "Used to be, they'd let us have a choice. Government took that away a long time ago. It's all just trouble, the whole thing." Then she waved her teacup toward us. "And double the trouble, mixing a breed of Earth females into our world who are always ripe."

"*I* knew this wasn't a good idea," I said.

Dor'is lowered her teacup. "You didn't want to come?"

I crossed my arms. "I just wanted to be a teacher."

"I argued, too," said Dor'is.

"So the Arway men are experiencing this affdesfals because of Karla and me?" Shandra asked.

Dor'is pursed her lips and shook her head. "Karla got away, but you shouldn't have been allowed to escape. That leaves one conclusion, but I'm only guessing."

"Guessing?"

"That you are with child."

Shandra gasped. She pressed her hands to her belly. "You think I'm pregnant?"

"You're here, instead of being torn apart in the fat one's barn. Reisan males are sensitive to hormone signatures. Not consciously, of course."

"I think Dar'el is," I said. "I think he knew this might happen."

Dor'is snorted. "He knew. Why do you think he was chosen?"

"So it was your decision," I said.

She shrugged. "The men were told Earth females could come, I tried to make the best of a bad situation. Dar'el has a faith that tempers him, and he could speak English. He's a smart one." She moved from the window and shuffled toward her little shelf of mysterious tins.

"You just said I should have been torn apart in Ra'nen's barn. How did you know we were there?" asked Shandra.

Dor'is set her teacup on the table. "Van'el is smart, too. And I had a good plan to control the initial hormonal response of the others."

"What plan?" I asked.

"I even concocted an elixir." She pulled the stopper on a small bottle and sniffed into it. "I can't imagine why it didn't work," she said, frowning at the container.

"Why what didn't work?" I asked, leaning forward to see if I could get a sniff of the bottle myself.

"Oh. Well, the elixir to impregnate you both as soon as possible," she said, without looking directly at me. "But it apparently hasn't worked in Dar'el's case."

Shandra coughed behind her hand.

I glared at her.

She drew up her feet onto the bed, hugged her knees, and smiled at me.

I turned my head to find Dor'is watching me. She bunched up her already-wrinkled brow and looked between Shandra and me in confusion.

"Oh, for crying out loud," I said. "Dar'el and I haven't consummated yet, okay? Not that it's anyone's business."

"He didn't mention any physical problems," said Dor'is.

"Look," I said, and stood up. I tugged at the hem of Dar'el's shirt and stalked toward Dor'is. "I'm sure there's nothing wrong with Dar'el. I just didn't want to. Did it never dawn on anyone I might not *want* to?"

Dor'is's eyes flashed with a Reisan blink. "No."

I threw up my hands and groaned.

"Are you saying," asked Dor'is, "…that despite being ripe, you chose against mating?"

"What a romantic way of putting it," I said.

"Why don't you just bless Karla and Dar'el?" asked Shandra. "Won't that eliminate all this confusion?"

"What would that do?" I asked.

Shandra stood and walked toward me. "A Nanayant

blessing marks a union as sacred. No other male would dare claim you then."

"That's so old-fashioned," said Dor'is.

"So are oil lanterns," I said.

"Tell me about it... ah, Shandra..." Dor'is darted out her green hand to touch Shandra's arm.

Shandra was peering beneath the gingham blanket at twisting, turning pipes. "What's this?"

"Don't touch it." Dor'is's face hardened.

Shandra tugged more blanket away. "But what is it? Looks like an old still." She smiled. "You brewing up home-grown kick-a-poo juice?"

Dor'is pulled the fabric from Shandra's hands and covered the pipes back over. "Yes, and I don't exactly want the whole village to know or they'll be banging on my door at all hours wanting some."

"You don't like wine?"

"Allergic," said Dor'is. "Now can we change the subject?"

"Yes, excuse me," I said. "We were talking about our many husbands and how I don't plan on sleeping my way through them. I'm leaving for the docking station in the morning."

"You'll only make things worse," said Dor'is.

"The men can have their money back. I'm going home."

"Look," said Dor'is. "You can't just leave now."

I marched toward the door. "So stop me."

"Don't go out there, Karla." Dor'is shuffled to follow me, and moments later I felt something pressing hard to my spine.

"What, are you threatening me?" I twisted, trying to look at whatever she was poking at my back.

"Dor'is?" asked Shandra's frightened voice.

"I can't let you go out there," said Dor'is.

A sharp jolt shot up my spine and rattled my brain. I tried to cry out, but everything went black.

I tried to move. Pain stabbed through my hips and thighs. My mouth was dry, and when I tried to open my eyes, they felt glued shut. Something was itchy against my back.

"Karla?" Shandra's voice. "Are you awake?"

I groaned.

"Don't move right away. Dor'is said you'll ache some."

"That witch shot me."

"I know."

"I guess the Repli-Chef isn't the only thing she smuggled in her flour sack."

Shandra's hand touched my shoulder. "She said it was for your own good. That if the men saw you they'd hurt you."

"And this feels so much better." I rolled to my side, and managed to peel my eyes open. I blinked at a fuzzy Shandra outline. "Where are we?"

"The Nanayant shack. Dor'is must have left while I was sleeping."

"What time is it?"

"I don't know. I can't find a clock or a sundial or anything."

I sat up on Dor'is's bed. A rush of nausea made me lean forward.

"Go slow," said Shandra. "I'd give you something out of the Nanayant's tins, but I don't know enough about herbs."

"There's likely rat poison or brain-washing drugs, anyway. I don't trust anything she's said."

"Why would she lie?"

"I don't know, Shandra, but I can't figure out why she'd shoot me, either."

"Because she was worried—"

"About what the sex-crazed Reisans would do to me. Yeah, I got that." I pushed to my feet. My eyesight was de-fuzzing and I could feel my legs again. I scuffled toward the door.

"It's locked," said Shandra.

"Did you try a window?"

"There's just the one. It doesn't open."

I scowled. "Sure, I'm seeing all kinds of reasons to trust her."

"She just wants to keep us safe."

"Or keep us prisoner." I turned to find Shandra sitting on the bed, her hands wringing. I realized it might be best to keep my opinions to myself for now. "You want something to eat? I could whip up some repli-eggs."

"Maybe."

"If you really are going to be a mom, you should keep up your strength."

Shandra smiled. "All right."

I made my way to the cupboard Dor'is had exposed last night, searching for the appliance. I yanked over a swatch of calico fabric. There it was, in all its shining glory, making me homesick. "What a relief," I said. The only thing I've really perfected on Dar'el's cooking stove is pancakes."

"I miss hot chocolate," said Shandra.

I knelt in front of the Repli-Chef and poked at the screen. "I hate when they change the programming. I can't find eggs."

"Try poultry. I think they moved eggs from the dairy section on the model three last year."

"Yeah, there it is." Then my hand paused. A realization crawled up my spine like a spider and tickled at the base of my brain. "Last year?"

"Maybe it was two years. I don't remember."

I twisted around to stare at Shandra. "But not six years. Didn't Dor'is say she smuggled this thing into her flour sack six years ago?"

"Yes, I think so." Shandra stood. She wandered toward the shelf of tins and began opening them. Then she touched the blanket covering the still. "Do you think she lied?"

"She's lying about something." I couldn't think why she'd have reason to, but that tingly sensation at the back of my head hadn't gone away. I sat on the floor, trying to puzzle it out. "She must keep contact with someone outside the village, but if so, why lie about it?"

"I've been wondering something, too." She yanked the blanket off the pipes and scowled, holding up a dried, puffy pellet the size of a lima bean. "If she's allergic to wine made of seeds, how can she drink anything made from them? And why doesn't she just program it into the Repli-Chef?"

I stood up and brushed at my backside. "What are you saying?"

"I don't know," said Shandra. "But look at this."

I walked toward her to see what she was pointing at. Looked to me like a brown, oblong box with skinny snakes coming out of it. Speckled snakes that dove together into the ground. "What?"

"Wires that go from that still into that battery, then into the ground." She touched a smooth panel on the wall. "And I'll bet this is a charge controller. And that…" She pointed toward a tiny patch of black material at the corner of the ceiling. "…is a solar plate."

I shrugged helplessly. "You lost me."

"What's a forgotten old woman in a shack in the outlands doing with photovoltaic equipment for brewing something that is not seed liquor?"

I couldn't think of an explanation. "How do you know about photo-whatever stuff?"

"I'm an ecological science tech. Though it doesn't take a scientist to see where our Earth is going." She held up a box of digital syringes. "What are these?"

Those I recognized. "Dosage administrators. We used them at the orphanage for inoculations, antibiotics.

Those look like a one-dose needle."

She set the box down. "Are the eggs burning?"

"I can replicook eggs without burning them!" I walked over and eyed the appliance again. "Besides, I haven't started them yet."

"Well, something's burning. Can't you smell it?"

I did smell it. Not like burned eggs, not even like smoke. More acrid. It stung the inside of my nose. "What is that?" I walked the room, sniffing and searching. At the fireplace, I found a fist-sized glass bulb leaking faint blue smog. "Some kind of firewood alternative?" I asked Shandra. But before she could answer, an explosion rocked the floor and knocked me flat. Heat billowed toward my face and chest, and I tried to roll over. My flesh stung all over like I was fighting off a swarm of bees.

I heard Shandra call my name. She tugged at my arms. The fireplace had become an orange wall of flame, and I stared at it while Shandra dragged me toward the door. "It's locked!" she said. She released me and ran past the fire to the kitchen window. She slammed an iron pot at the glass. She grabbed the chair and tried that. "It won't break!" Her voice was high and her face panicked.

I was trying to think through my own fear, but I could only stare in pain and confusion. The fire growled at the roof, then leapt out to swallow it. Orange flames turned yellow and crept across a ceiling beam toward me. Shandra called for me again.

At the sound of my name, I snapped aware.

My hands grappled at the hinges of the door, trying to wrench out the nail, but it didn't budge. Shandra dropped to her knees beside me with a kitchen knife and pried at it. I peered up at the ceiling. The fire roiled directly over our heads.

Then a voice shouted through the door. "Amna tet!" Knuckles rapped hard on the wood. It sounded very much like the yellow-eyed sumo wrestler.

"We're here!" cried Shandra, and pounded back. "Eshua ay arwanen!"

"Trenet!" said the voice.

Shandra yanked at my shoulder. "Get back."

The door splintered. Green arms reached through, then a round face with yellow eyes. I shrank back, but Ra'nen's hand found my shirt collar and pulled. I scraped through the broken door and flopped over the man's shoulder. With a grunt, he tugged at Shandra, and she got tossed over his other shoulder.

I thought I'd be relieved to be free of the fire, but I was Ra'nen's captive. I seriously considered jumping back in. Unfortunately, I didn't have the strength. My face sizzled, my arms ached, and I was too tired to fight.

"Don't be scared," whispered Shandra.

Too late, I thought, as I felt my eyes flutter closed.

I heard voices like people were speaking gibberish through an air bubble. Someone pressed something cold to my face. I felt like I'd been through this before, but couldn't remember quite what it was I'd been through.

I opened my eyes to find Ra'nen staring down at me. I sat up fast, and nearly cracked my forehead against his nose. A cold cloth dropped to my lap.

"Where am I?" I asked. Yellow light leaked through wall slats. Hay dust floated like tiny fairies through the brightness. Near the ceiling, I heard a bird flutter from a corner roost. Ra'nen's barn.

Shandra offered me a cup of water, her face smudged with soot. "Ra'nen says the shack is destroyed. It's still smoking."

"Where's Dar'el?" I glared at Ra'nen. "What did you do to him?"

Just then the barn door roared open and pounding feet rumbled over the floor. "Shandra!" I heard Van'el say. Shandra hopped to her feet. Van'el's hands stretched out from a crowd of green arms and hugged her tightly.

Reisan men stood around the pair, voices strained, words spilling over others' words. Van'el murmured into Shandra's ear, and she turned to look at me, her eyes soft and rimmed with pity.

"What's wrong?" I asked. " Where's Dar'el? What's going on?"

Ra'nen laid his plump hand on my knee.

"Don't even think about it," I snarled. He didn't understand my words, but he must have read my face. He withdrew his hand.

"Karla, no one has seen Dar'el since last night." Shandra knelt at my side. "The men have been looking for him. He hasn't been home."

"They've been looking for him?" I wiggled around, trying to get to my knees. "They're the ones who ran him off! Came to our house all pumped up on affdesfals, trying to hurt him!" I finally got to my feet and balled my fists.

Van'el took my shoulders. "Dar'el was not hurt. He fought hard, his eyes as full of affdesfals as the others. He lost himself, almost killed Esh'al and Car'lis."

"What?"

He sighed. "The others came to their senses. Dar'el did not. Even I ran. I was afraid of him."

"You're crazy. He wouldn't do that." I looked down to Ra'nen, over to Shandra, and then to the group of men who stood silently and watched us. For the first time I noticed small bandages around the tips of ears, tied to shoulders, and clinging to various noses. "This place is crazy. Everyone's lying; everyone's trying to hurt each other. The Nanayant shot me! And she tried to burn Shandra and me in her shack!"

Van'el looked down at Ra'nen. The giant Reisan pushed to his feet and lumbered toward me. "Saw no Nanayant. Only Dar'el."

"What are you saying?"

"Saw only Dar'el."

Shandra came beside me. "Van'el, you don't think Dar'el started that fire, do you?"

"He couldn't have," I said. "It started inside. *Inside.* The glass bulb exploded. Look at me." I stuck out my arms, the sleeves of Dar'el's shirt pinpricked with tiny holes.

"Maybe he came in while we were sleeping," said Shandra.

"The door was locked!"

"Maybe he locked it afterward."

I stared at Shandra. "Dar'el didn't shoot me in the back and lock me in. He didn't lie about the Repli-Chef."

"Repli-Chef?" asked Van'el.

I pressed my fingertips to my aching eyes. "Dor'is told us she smuggled a Repli-Chef in a flour sack six years ago when she came here, but the model is too new to be six years old."

Van'el raised his brows to Shandra. "What does that mean?"

Shandra shrugged. "I'm not sure, but it's not the only thing she lied about. And when she was explaining affdesfals to us, she mentioned me being attacked in this barn, even though I didn't say where."

"But why would the Nanayant want to hurt you?"

"Why would Dar'el?" I asked, lowering my hands to look into Van'el's black eyes.

"Not to share human girl," grumbled Ra'nen. He gripped my hips and pulled me back against himself. "Aya may varna turret tay."

I wobbled against his gelatinous belly. "If you don't stop grabbing me, I'll varna your turret tay, all right." I stomped onto the arch of his foot.

He howled and gave me a push.

The group of men behind him shifted feet and exchanged looks. One of them nodded at Van'el, as though urging him to speak. Shandra saw it, too, because she touched Van'el's arm. "What is it?"

"We do not know what it means," he said. "But we have been speaking of things since last night, and…"

"What?" I asked, too irritated to be patient.

"It seems the Nanayant told each of the others in secret that you both were to be theirs during the barn celebration." Van'el swallowed tightly.

"What?" I asked again, able only to echo a single syllable.

"But," Shandra flustered. "But, she… she said she was trying to protect us from affdesfals! She even gave you and Dar'el an elixir to help us get pregnant, to buy us some time!"

"Well, she lied again," I said. "What a surprise." I pushed through the men and headed for the door, so much anger churning inside my stomach it was making me ill.

"There must be some mistake," said Shandra.

I stopped and whirled to face her. "Isn't it obvious? She said she didn't want us here, and that showing how dangerous the exchange could be might stop the program altogether. Think about it, Shandra."

"You mean, you think she… did it on purpose?"

I looked at Van'el, who wasn't arguing. "*Hoping* for affdesfals," I said. "Encouraging it. Which probably has a lot more to do with that elixir she gave you than anything to protect Shandra and me."

Van'el's gaze tightened with pain, and he looked downward. "I drank the medicine. I believed her."

"Of course you did," said Shandra. She took his hand and kissed his knuckles. "We all did."

"Speak for yourself," I said. I turned and kicked open the door. "I'm going to the processing station to get the money back. Then I'm going home." I stalked out of the barn and toward Dar'el's house to change into my dress.

When I reached the front door, I paused. The cascading pink flowers rustled against the roof, catching my attention. The breeze carried their scent to me. Vanilla spice. I thought of Mama Iris then, and the tea she used to brew while we talked of teaching, or children, or dreams. But, did we talk of dreams? I was certain we had. I just couldn't recall whatever they'd been.

No matter. I would be back on Earth soon, and I would think of new ones.

I made my way through the house to the bedroom. I caught my reflection as I passed a mirror, and sucked in a breath. I had twigs in my hair. Tiny burn spatters dotted my forehead and nose and were beginning to scab. The collar of Dar'el's shirt was torn off, and a scrape across my collarbone was crispy with dried blood. Unbelievable. This place *was* trying to kill me, and I'd only been here a few days.

I turned my back to the mirror and pulled at the shirt buttons. I hadn't realized my fingers were shaking until I tried to make them work. Finally the filthy cloth dropped to the floor. I stepped into my yellow dress, smoothed it up my arms, and then struggled with the tiny fasteners at my throat.

I heard a muffled thump. The sound came through the open window, so I peered outside. The door of the shed was partially open. I heard another noise like something being dragged. Definitely inside the shed. I ducked through the window and crept toward the sound.

I pulled open the shed door. Sunlight cascaded in around me and illuminated a green figure hunched on the floor in a corner, with his hands gripped into his dark green dreadlocks.

"Dar'el?"

He looked up quickly. "Go, Karla. Go away."

"Are you all right?"

"No. I am not safe, please go."

I watched him, thinking I should leave, but unable to.

"Do not come closer. I am begging you," he said, his voice strained.

"I'm not afraid." I was surprised to realize I meant it. I knelt beside him. "Van'el said you lost your temper last night."

He pressed his elbows to his raised knees and touched the heels of his hands to his forehead. He turned away from me.

"It wasn't your fault," I said.

He shook his head. "I am an animal. I am no better than the rest."

"You're no animal."

He turned his face toward mine. "I thought I could

control it. I thought I was stronger." He looked down toward his hands. "But I am weak. I let it take my mind."

"It's built into you, Dar'el. You're Reisan. You can't expect to fight your very nature."

"Yes I can. I am more than my nature!" He slapped his hand to the floor, but then hissed out a breath of pain.

"Are you hurt?" I took his hand and turned it. His palm was dark and blistered. "Did you burn yourself?"

He yanked his hand away from me.

"You need to tend to that. And don't let the others see it. They already suspect you started the fire."

He looked at my face again. His expression slowly clouded.

"But you didn't," I said, eyeing him.

He shook his head. "I do not remember. God help me, Karla, but I do not remember."

"How can you not?"

He continued to shake his head. "It took my mind. I was enraged, and I wanted to protect you. I remember the others afraid of me. And I wanted to find you, but I could not have you, and I was trying to think through a fog of such anger." He began trembling. I touched his shoulder.

"You wouldn't hurt me, Dar'el. No matter how angry."

"But I was there. I do remember fire, and I... I was searching."

"You did say you wanted to protect me."

I could tell he didn't believe me. For a minute,

I actually doubted too, but it didn't last. I smiled, and cupped his face in my hands. "I trust you."

Tears welled in his blue eyes. He placed his hands over mine and smiled, very faintly. The heat of his burned palms invaded my own skin, and I wondered how he was managing the pain. "Will you show me how to tend to your burns?" I asked.

He nodded. His gaze was soft, and it slowly settled onto my mouth.

I drew in my bottom lip, very aware he was staring at me. I grew warmer, and realized the heat wasn't coming from his palms, but from his eyes. Then he leaned toward me, slowly. I sensed his kiss in the air between us.

I knelt mutely in place, caught between retreat and surrender. Would a kiss make it easier for me to leave, or harder? There was only one way to know. I closed my eyes and let it come.

But it didn't. Moments later, I reopened my eyes to find his face inches from mine, his jaw tightly clenched. Then he turned his head, released my hands, and pushed to stand.

"Dar'el?"

"I am taking you to the processing station."

"Right now?" I stood and brushed wood chips away from my knees.

"As soon as you are ready."

"What about your hands?"

"I will be fine." He wasn't looking at me as he made his way to the door. "I will not risk you any longer.

Gather your things and meet me out front. I will drive the carriage myself." He closed the shed door behind himself.

I followed him out, but he was gone. I went back through the bedroom window to find my things as he told me, but only stood beside the bed, staring around the room. Nothing here belonged to me. Except for the reshka he gave me, which was laying on the chair. I picked it up, hugged it to my chest, and cast a final look to the room.

Outside, the sky had turned milky white and smelled of rain. The carriage was waiting at the road, with Dar'el in the driving seat. "I would have liked to tell Shandra goodbye," I said, as I hurried toward him.

"You wish to take the time?" he asked. The burgundy horse-beast whinnied.

I did wish, but got the distinct impression he didn't. I climbed the steps of the carriage and sat down inside, feeling I was a nuisance to be secretly rid of. In my daydreams of leaving Arway and Reisas, I hadn't imagined the part where Dar'el would be so eager to see me off.

The journey dragged on. Wet blobs of rainfall began to slap against the carriage window. By the time we pulled into place outside the processing center, the sky was alabaster pale and quietly rumbling.

The carriage door opened, held by Dar'el, whose dreadlocks dripped with water. His shirt was so soggy it had become transparent. "Think it'll rain?" I asked, in the hopes of lightening things. It didn't.

Dar'el hadn't spoken by the time we stepped inside. Not even by the time we'd reached the outer office. When he did talk, it was to the scrawny male receptionist behind a lacquered half-wall. "Ragin Dar'el Karla esh tuant tet eskatay."

The receptionist looked up. When he spotted me, his eyes slowly rose to stare at my face, and then my hair. His expression drew Dar'el's eyes to me, too.

Dar'el softened, regarding me. He removed a small twig from above my ear, and smoothed my hair into place. He shook his head, and opened his mouth to speak, but then a door behind the desk whispered open to reveal a hallway, and he looked away. "I will explain things," said Dar'el. "Wait here for me."

He stepped into the hallway without looking back. I watched him leave a trail of wet boot prints on the glistening floor and wondered if anyone would mind if I cried a little.

Then I heard voices coming from another door to my left. I couldn't understand the words, but one of the speakers had a shriveled tone that seemed familiar. I glanced at the receptionist, who was talking into some kind of mouthpiece affixed to his chin. So I tiptoed toward that door.

I listened for a moment, and wished I'd taken the time to learn some basics of their language. I turned the knob and swung open the door just a little to peer through the crack. All I could see was a stocky male with a shrubbery for hair. He waved his hand toward the other babbling voice, and produced a dosage administrator from an inside pocket of his suit. A gnarled hand snatched at it.

"Ragin Karla?" asked a voice behind me. I turned to find the receptionist with his thin arms crossed, eyeing me. He stepped toward me, reached around my arm for the door handle, and pulled the thing closed.

"Whose office is this?" I asked.

He narrowed his eyes.

"Nanayant Elt Dor'is?"

"Please take seat," he said, sweeping his arm toward the lobby.

"I need to speak with someone in charge about the Arway Nanayant," I said.

Then I felt the door handle turn against my back, and heard a click. The door opened, and I caught sight of a dark eye staring from a wrinkled, honeydew melon face. It was Dor'is!

She gasped, and the door slammed shut. Before I could react, I heard the lock twist. "I know what you did, Dor'is!" I said, just in case she thought she could get away with it. I grabbed the receptionist's scrawny arms. "Does that office have a window?"

He made no sound, only gaped his mouth and widened his eyes.

"Window?" I repeated. Still nothing. "Never mind." I ran toward the main doors to find out myself. I pushed them open and stumbled out into daylight that only days ago had blinded me.

My first step was into a puddle of rainwater that splashed my dress. I turned the corner, and spotted

Dor'is climbing, legs-first, through the side of the cement building.

"Oh, no, you don't!" I hollered. I ran across the lawn toward the window, mud spraying with each step. I felt it hit my cheeks. I tasted it on my lips. When I got close enough to reach her, she was out the window and trying to escape, all hobble and hunchback. I tackled her.

There was a feeble cry from someone through the window. I heard footfalls behind me—several pairs of feet—and then Dar'el's shout. "Karla!"

"Help me, Dar'el," I said. Dor'is was struggling beneath me, less of a weakling than I'd guessed.

"Why are you on the Nanayant?" he asked when he got close enough. He tugged me off her, but I held tight, yanking at the shoulders of her voluminous and muddy robe. She came to her feet, too, pulling out of the mud with a slurp.

"Don't let her get away, Dar'el, she tried to kill Shandra and me!"

"Ragin Karla?" asked another Reisan who swept in behind Dar'el. Something about the way this one held his shoulders made him tower over us all, even Dar'el, though when I looked closely, he wasn't really taller than anyone.

"Installation Director Arness," explained Dar'el.

I released Dor'is. I straightened a little and tried to smooth my hair, but when gray sludge plopped onto my shoulder from my fingers, I figured I still looked pretty disastrous. "Dor'is was trying to escape," I explained.

"Escape?" asked the director.

Dor'is pointed at me. "This human attacked me without reason."

"You were climbing out a window!"

"And so I deserve to be ambushed?"

"Please calm down," said the director, holding up his hand. "And Elt Vik'ay, I see you there in the window, please come out."

The shape in the window shifted and emerged, becoming the young man with bushy hair I'd seen in the office. He gingerly stepped out onto the wet ground and then stared at me with round, green eyes. And he blinked. A real blink, with eyelids.

"Now, someone explain to me what is going on." The director looked at Dar'el, but Dar'el just looked at me.

"I… ah…" I looked back at the youth, distracted by his eyes. "Who…?"

"Elt Vik'ay," said the director. "Immigration assistant."

When I glanced back at the director, I realized by his pursed lips he was waiting on me. In fact, everyone was looking at me. "Dor'is started a fire in her cabin," I began. "She locked me and Shandra inside and set off something to explode."

"Nonsense," said Dor'is, and spun to walk away.

Dar'el clutched the woman's shoulder. "Just a minute."

Dor'is snorted. "You started that fire, Dar'el. You knew the women were in my shack. I tried to stop you, but you were so crazy with affdesfals, you struck me and

I was helpless to stop you. Look at his hands," she said, jutting out her chin toward the director. "Ask him how he burned himself."

"Dar'el wouldn't hurt me," I said, my fists balling. I was considering striking her myself, but the receptionist was making his way toward us with a Reisan in a maroon uniform. We were apparently drawing a crowd.

"One of your townspeople burned your shack with women inside, and you decided it wasn't worth reporting?" asked the director.

Dor'is narrowed her dark eyes. "I was here to do just that."

"That's not all she did," I said. I stepped forward. "She set up Shandra and me to be attacked by the Arway men. I think she was trying to get us hurt because she doesn't like the exchange program."

"What do you mean she set you up?" asked Dar'el.

I lowered my voice and leaned toward him. "Last night, in the barn. The others said she'd told them each secretly it was supposed to be their turn with us."

"Olai shay," he said, and glared at her. Then he pushed her toward the director. "I believe there is cause for investigation," he said. "If Karla says Dor'is tried to hurt her, it is the truth."

"Ridiculous!" Dor'is struggled to pull loose from Dar'el's grip. "She's a hormonal Earth outcast. She's the one who wants to sabotage the program."

"And yet you were the one who informed the men of Arway they were to share the two Earth females, were you not?" asked the director.

Dor'is stopped struggling. She met the director's eyes, but she seemed smaller. "I felt it was the best solution at—"

"Despite clear guidelines. Despite knowing the consequences."

"Oh, what is the big deal? It's not as though this is about free choice, is it?" Dor'is waved her hand toward me. "She was brought here to reproduce. Your bureaucratic guidelines and tasteful manners can't conceal that this exchange program is just cattle-driving."

I was startled to discover Dor'is and I agreed on something. I almost said so, but she kept talking.

"What difference does it make to you who she mates with? What difference does it make to her? It's what she's made for, isn't it?" She waved her hand at me again, and her face curled inward. "Look at her. It's disgusting."

I was ready to slug her this time, despite the onlookers. I made a move toward her, but Dar'el put his hand on my shoulder.

"Fine," said Dor'is. "Maybe I nudged it along a little, but what happened was inevitable. Because you won't leave well enough alone. Meddling in the affairs of my body, taking away my choices. Now you're meddling again with Earthlings." She pulled back her shoulders, and her stooped back creaked when she tried to straighten. "Hasn't it dawned on anyone that maybe we're all trying just a little too hard?"

"Too hard?" asked the director.

"Maybe Reisas and Earth are two civilizations whose time has come. We should fade out with dignity, not with all this scrabbling to create a whole new creature that was obviously never intended to exist."

The young Reisan sucked in a sharp breath. "Ayantamel!" He touched his fingers to his mouth.

Dor'is startled. "Vik'ay, esta tu ah…"

"What are they saying?" I asked Dar'el. "What's Ayantamel?"

"Grandmother," said Dar'el.

"Speak in English, please," said the director. "Both of you."

"Is that what you really think of me, Grandmother?" asked the Reisan. I could see moisture in his green eyes.

Dor'is shrank inside her robe, looking fragile and tired. "I didn't mean you, Vik'ay."

"Yes, you did." He stalked toward Dor'is. "I think you've meant all along for me to never have children." Then he turned to face the director, his boots squishy on the gray mud. "But I want to have children. I do. I just… I let her talk me into…"

The director put a hand on the young man's shoulder. "Into what?"

"Shut up, Vik'ay," said Dor'is.

The young man looked toward his muddy boots. Then he turned and reached into Dor'is's robes. Dor'is batted at his hands, but he withdrew a small dosage administrator and offered it toward the director.

The director took in a sharp breath this time. Dar'el's eyes narrowed.

"Is this…?" asked the director. He squeezed a drop of pink liquid onto his fingertip and dabbed it to his tongue. Then he looked at Dor'is. "Trestakaya." He clenched his teeth. He looked at the uniformed officer and nodded toward Dor'is. "Lock her in the recovery room until she can be properly transported."

"Nanayant Elt Dor'is, you are under arrest for the attempted murder of Ragin Karla and Baren Shandra," said Dar'el, coming from behind me to grasp the old woman's arms. "And for possession of Trestakaya contraband."

"This is crazy! You can't arrest me!" Dor'is struggled, and Dar'el nearly lifted her off her feet to pass her to the uniformed officer. She continued to wrestle and yell, lapsing into Reisan. For such a wiry little shrew, she really gave the uniform trouble. Vik'ay, on the other hand, lumbered off quietly behind.

"Please cooperate, Vik'ay, and I will see to it you are handled gently," said the director.

"You will have to tell me everything that happened in that cabin, Karla," said Dar'el. "What was said, what was seen. Shandra, too. A full statement."

"Statement?" I asked.

"We will need to seal off the remains of the shack," he told the director. "The brewing system mentioned by Baren Shandra must be how Dor'is was manufacturing it."

"So a fire could have a double purpose. To destroy whatever evidence was inside, and to remove those who had seen it."

"All during the confusion of affdesfals, so we would not be able to recall details afterward. Nearly perfect," said Dar'el.

"Maybe you two would be more impressed if I'd actually died."

Dar'el looked at me, his blue eyes wide. "Karla, I did not mean—"

"Well, what did you mean? When did you talk to Shandra? And why do you suddenly sound like a policeman?"

"Ragin Dar'el was a police officer in Mau'ana, our capital, before he was wounded," said the director. "He volunteered for a rural settlement eight years ago."

He shook his head. "I came to Arway to get away from violence." Then he stepped toward the director and touched the man's elbow to guide him along the building. "We should get that evidence to safety."

"It is fortuitous you were a witness." The director stepped across the mud without so much as dirtying the tips of his cloth shoes. He held the dosage administrator with two fingertips, as though it contained Black Death.

I fell in behind them, my own feet sinking so deeply into muck I strained with every step. "What evidence? What is Trestakay?"

"Trestakaya," the director corrected. "It is a synthetic hormone that suppresses female ripening. The chemical has been banned for many years, ever since we learned its prolonged use affected following generations, making them unable to reproduce."

"You mean that's why your people are dying out

with no babies to replace them?" I asked. "Because of a drug?"

"A synthetic hormone," he said. He paused and looked over his shoulder at me. "Reisas has a complicated past, Ragin Karla. Trestakaya is an unfortunate product of that." He regarded me for a long moment, and then faced forward and continued walking toward the building's main doors. "I have no experience with this sort of illegal activity, Dar'el, I will need your advice as to proceedings."

"There will be an investigation as to whether she was manufacturing it for personal use or whether she and her granddaughter were trafficking."

"Granddaughter?" I asked.

"Elt Vik'ay." The director nodded toward the doors where the rabble had disappeared inside.

I blinked. I'd thought Vik'ay was a male.

"Your wife will cooperate with our legalities?" asked the director, pausing again. One hand rested on the carved handle of the main door, one hand cradled the dosage administrator.

Wife. "No one told me I was supposed to be a wife to all those men," I said, remembering again. Getting angry again.

"Ah, yes… about that." The director removed his hand from the door and faced me. "A grievous misunderstanding. And we are already working to make amends. Your return passage to Earth will be at no expense to you, or to the men of Arway."

"What about bringing more women? Ones who

really want to come?" I asked.

The director smiled thinly. "That would be an expensive prospect."

"As costly as having an illegal Trestakaya plant operating under your very nose in Arway, where the venerated Nanayant attempted to slaughter the first two women of the union program within days of their arrival?"

His jaw clenched. He cleared his throat. "Yes, well. I'm sure something can be arranged."

Then the main door opened, and Shandra's smiling face peeked out. "Don't forget the blessing," she said.

"Shandra!"

"Shall we join them in the lobby?" asked the director, sweeping his hand toward the door. I watched that hand, and the graceful way his fingers met the air. Then it dawned on me. He was a female!

How many females had I'd come across without recognizing them? I glanced toward Dar'el. Could Reisan males tell the difference? Or did the hormones confuse them, too?

"Isn't it exciting?" squealed Shandra, yanking me through the door and pulling me into a tight hug. Van'el stood behind her, his green hand on her shoulder. The director brushed past us, speaking quietly to Dar'el. They both continued into the lobby.

I returned Shandra's hug. "I thought I wasn't going to be able to say goodbye."

She released me. She looked over her shoulder at Dar'el, then back to me. "You mean you're still leaving?"

Well, wasn't I?

"Didn't they tell you?" asked Shandra. "They've made me interim Nanayant." She leaned in to whisper in my ear. "I really put my foot down. You would have been proud of me."

"That's great," I said.

"I know! And as my first official act I'm going to bless you two in front of the whole village."

"You don't have to do that," I said. "I won't be here long enough to need it."

"Actually," said Van'el. "We have been told the next passage to Earth is planned in three months."

"Three months?" I blinked. "Three months?"

"Although, I am not certain how the legal proceedings will affect this. You may be asked to stay longer."

I must have looked faint, because Van'el braced his arm around my back. "But Dar'el has asked us to provide our home for you in the meantime. We are happy to, of course."

"Unless you'd rather stay with Dar'el," said Shandra, smiling faintly, her brows suggestively arched.

I looked toward the man who was my husband. He continued to speak with the director. He held open a brown envelope, and when the director carefully slid the dosage administrator inside, Dar'el folded the flap and wrapped string around the entire thing. Then he pointed toward the receptionist and other office personnel, and gave them orders I didn't understand. I watched him for a few minutes, but he never looked to find me.

"No," I said, and wearily turned for the door. "I'll go with you."

Shandra exchanged a look with Van'el. I could feel her disappointment, but she just nodded. "First thing we'll do is get you a bath." She took my hand and led me toward the doors. "It'll make you feel better."

"Sounds great," I said, knowing I needed one; knowing she was right about my outsides. But I was pretty sure it wasn't going to make me feel any better on the inside.

I knelt in Shandra's garden, my shins cradled by soft loam. The *zrrt-za* of green-black beetles and the whistling report of the pastel-feathered birds that hunted them had become a familiar morning opus. I'd learned this patch of ground. I'd cleared weeds and old leaves, had made room for foliage to stretch and breathe, had watched time pass in the unfolding of buds into frumpy petals.

I counted petals now. On the daisy-like flower in front of me, only one had fallen. When they all dropped, it would be nearly time to shuttle home.

Home. The word had lost its meaning.

"This garden likes you better than it does me," said Shandra, crossing the yard toward me, calico fabric folded over one arm, and a parchment note in her hand. "I could never tell the difference between flowers and weeds. I think I kept pulling the wrong ones."

I smiled. "They do look the same at first."

She held up the parchment. "We've been summoned again. Next week."

I looked up and shielded the sun with my hand. "Again? What for?"

She parted the note at the fold with her thumb and read. "A bureau deciding about Dor'is's mental state."

"What's to decide? She's crazy."

Shandra smiled. "Well, true. But maybe it's the Trestakaya. Van'el told me one of the long-term effects of the drug—"

"Synthetic hormone," I said, waving my finger, grinning and scolding at the same time.

"Right. Synthetic hormone. I guess it causes a kind of aggression similar to affdesfals." She stepped into the garden, walking cautiously between rows of tidy foliage.

I didn't find that hard to believe. "But Dor'is doesn't need any help being aggressive, I'm sure of that. And I'll be happy to tell the bureau."

"You're probably right." She paused near me, her bare toes the same color as the garden soil. "Her family is likely to say the same thing. She and her son had a falling out when he married a human, but they weren't very close even before that."

I pushed to my feet. "Have you heard what's going to happen to Vik'ay?"

"Not officially, but Dar'el says they won't charge her with anything. She's cooperating. Plus..." She smiled. "Either Dor'is's Trestakaya was a mild version of the original, or it wasn't having the same effect on Vik'ay's blended DNA. She might as well have been feeding

Vik'ay cough syrup."

I laughed. "I would have liked to see Dor'is's reaction to that news."

"Me too."

"So maybe human DNA really will be an answer for Riesas," I said.

Shandra drew in a deep breath, and the calico fabric over her arm fluttered as she pressed her hand to her belly. Her dark eyes radiated, and I could feel the warmth of her smile even beneath the midday sun. "I'd like to think I'm an answer. And that my child will be."

I regarded her, wondering if I should be envious of her contentment. All I could feel was happiness for her. "You're going to be a great mom."

"So are you, someday."

I hadn't thought of myself that way before. Considering it startled me. I awkwardly stabbed my finger toward the fabric on her arm. "What's that you have?"

"A dress. For you." She held it up, letting the skirt of it touch the flower petals. The pink of the pattern was an exact match.

"From Dar'el?" He'd been sending a dress a week for the last several weeks.

"He likes taking care of you, I think," she said. She laid the dress against my hands, and I accepted it. "He misses you, Karla."

"He said that?"

"He doesn't have to." She bent and touched the face of a daisy. "Just like you never say how much you miss him, but you do."

I touched my left earlobe with my free hand. I'd wrenched out the metal clasp a while ago, but an irritated scab remained, and it stung. "I miss Mama Iris, too, but I don't exactly want to be her wife."

She laughed, and tugged at the flower's stem. I moved to stop her, but the stem snapped. I watched her slide the daisy—my daisy—behind her ear. "So what do you want?"

I held up the dress to examine it. I had five others, all similar in style, with rounded collars and delicate buttons near the neck. "I don't know," I said, even though I'd been pondering that question on my own for a long time.

"Karla?" I recognized Dar'el's voice immediately, and lowered the dress to discover him standing in Shandra's doorway. He was wearing a blue flannel shirt, like the last time I'd seen him, and it lit the blue of his oval eyes. His hands were clasped around a small box.

Shandra was right. I missed him.

"Oh, I need to check on the…" Shandra scuffled through the garden row and toward the door. "…something in the kitchen." She glanced over her shoulder at me, briefly, before ducking behind Dar'el and disappearing.

He was regarding my face. When I realized his eyes were on me, I took a step toward him. "I like this new dress you've given me."

He smiled. "Do you? The pink pattern made me think of you."

"Yes, it's very pretty. Thank you."

"You're welcome."

I returned his smile. And then I folded the dress and laid it over my arm, because I'd run out of things to say.

His smile faded, and he stepped out of the doorway. "I came to tell you I've been offered a job in the city. In Mau'ana."

"A job?"

"I would be reinstated as a police officer. Since I have been working on your case, I have made contact again with several former colleagues."

"I see." I meant to tell him congratulations, but I couldn't bring myself to say it. "So you're leaving Arway?"

"Yes. I… thought it might… that you would wish that." He looked toward his hands, and the box within them. "I have amended the paperwork so the home here is yours."

"You're giving me your house?"

"And I will arrange things so you will not go without." I opened my mouth to reply, but he held up his hand. "I do not wish for you to return to Earth and its sickness. If my leaving will make you stay, I will provide for you from Mau'ana."

I was struck silent. I tried to sort through my thoughts and feelings, searching for a reply. The best I could manage was, "Why?"

"You are my wife," he said, his words soft. "It is the least I can do."

"Do you mean… it is the least you can do for me? Or the most?" I tried smiling.

He did smile, very faintly. Then he stepped toward me, his gaze steady on my face. "I could do more."

I believed him. The thought made my knees weaken. In that moment, I knew if he tried to kiss me, I wouldn't resist.

He only took my hand. He pushed fabric away from my palm and set the small box onto it. He didn't speak another word; he only stared into my eyes. Then he eased back, and turned.

I watched him walk away until he disappeared around the side of Shandra's house. Then, with a trembling hand, I ran my fingers over the small box. It was barely larger than a walnut, the wood dark and smooth. Tiny leaves cascaded from the upper left corner, across the front, and faded at the bottom right corner. They looked so real, I had to touch them again.

Shandra peered at me through the window by the door. Then she reappeared in the doorway, and gripped her skirt with her hands to hurry toward me. "Well? What happened? What did he say?"

"He gave me something," I said, feeling emotion in the back of my throat tightening my words.

"A gift? Let me see." She eased the box from my fingers and pried it open. Then her brow wrinkled, and she held the pieces toward me. "There's nothing inside."

I laughed a little, because I was so near to crying. "The gift *is* the box," I said. "But that isn't what I meant."

"Then what did he give you?" she asked.

I smiled. "A choice."

More from Big Imagine

Free Booklet!

with newsletter signup

Super! Strange

*Secret Powers of
Quirky Thinkers*

A scientifically-backed scoop
on introversion and highly
sensitive people (HSPs) by
Jackie Gamber.

Join the Newsletter

Stay up to date on book and film projects, swag, and exclusive articles only geeks could love. And maybe a secret handshake.

bigimagine.com/newsletter

# More from Big Imagine

Read the Blog

From one scifi nerd to another, Jackie blogs for you about kick-ass stories, developing outrageous imagination, and feeding the geek in our gray matter.

bigimagine.com/blog

Explore our Films

Big Imagine doesn't only publish books. We make movies, too! Our film projects are circulating in festivals and are offered on streaming sites. We'd love to have you as a supporter!

bigimagine.com/films